# THE NAKED ISLAND

D1004886

# The Naked Island

A NOVEL

Bryna Wasserman

KEY PORTER BOOKS

Copyright © 2004 by Bryna Wasserman

All rights reserved. No part of this work covered by the copyrights hereon may be reproduced or used in any form or by any means—graphic, electronic or mechanical, including photocopying, recording, taping or information storage and retrieval systems—without the prior written permission of the publisher, or, in case of photocopying or other reprographic copying, a licence from Access Copyright, the Canadian Copyright Licensing Agency, One Yonge Street, Suite 1900, Toronto, Ontario, M6B 3A9.

**National Library of Canada Cataloguing in Publication Data**

Wasserman, Bryna
    The naked island : a novel / Bryna Wasserman.

ISBN 1-55263-638-0

I. Title.

PS8645.A88N33 2004        C813'.6        C2004-903535-5

The Canada Council for the Arts | Le Conseil des Arts du Canada since 1917 | depuis 1957

ONTARIO ARTS COUNCIL
CONSEIL DES ARTS DE L'ONTARIO

The publisher gratefully acknowledges the support of the Canada Council for the Arts and the Ontario Arts Council for its publishing program. We acknowledge the support of the Government of Ontario through the Ontario Media Development Corporation's Ontario Book Initiative.

We acknowledge the financial support of the Government of Canada through the Book Publishing Industry Development Program (BPIDP) for our publishing activities.

Key Porter Books Limited
70 The Esplanade
Toronto, Ontario
Canada M5E 1R2

www.keyporter.com

Lyrics from *Who the Cap Fit* on page 45, written by Carleton Barrett and Aston Barrett © 1976 Fifty Six Hope Road / Odnil Music Limited (ASCAP). All rights administered in North and South America by Fairwood Music USA (ASCAP) on behalf of Blue Mountain Music, Ltd.; all rights for the rest of the world administered by Fairwood Music, Ltd. (PRS) on behalf of Blue Mountain Music, Ltd. Used with permission.

Text design: Peter Maher
Electronic formatting: Jean Lightfoot Peters

Printed and bound in Canada

04 05 06 07 08 5 4 3 2 1

*For my mother
and for my father
Gloria & Marvin Wasserman*

Selves which are coherent, seamless, bounded, and whole
are indeed illusions.
DORINNE K. KONDO

Let's say evil exists. It has no form. No identity. It breathes by seducing souls. Survives by feeding on the life force of those who are smitten by its captivating presence. Rachel was one of those souls. She had thought when evil was near there would be a sign, like the shadows one feels on a tree-lined street at night. Having been influenced by books and movies, she would recognize by a chill down her neck the insidious trembling of evil as it closed in on the lights.

But on her journey to find her home Kifli Talib stepped in front of Rachel and she lost her way.

# *Prologue*

In 1787, on the morning of the new moon in July, Joseph Brant, a Mohawk chief, was fording the flooded banks of the Grand River on his way to Lake Erie. On the same day, the Dutch in Java murdered the Indonesian priest Qadar. This is as good a place as any for me to begin.

Then the story sleeps for one hundred years, being nothing but the harvests in the fields until 1887 when three seemingly unrelated events occurred: the Armenian Sarkies brothers opened Raffles Hotel in Singapore, a farmhouse was built at Evans Point on the shore of Lake Erie, and in Java, Zulkanyan, a descendant of the slain priest Qadar, suddenly died when a curse he had set against his neighbours reversed and killed him instead. The leaves he had used to cast the spell were overturned. Zulkanyan called out to Qadar but no help came to him. His body was found floating in a river. His soul set out wandering.

These happenings would have remained disconnected if

the spirit of Zulkanyan hadn't crossed the water and in 1957 arrived at the wide spaces of the wheat fields where the Mohawk had trod. He appeared while I was looking down my well checking the waterline. I smiled, remembering how my beloved wife Rachel had always said it was going to rain and the well would fill, not to worry.

I was getting married again that Saturday and was missing Rachel, which made me vulnerable when Zulkanyan swept in. He introduced himself by covering the house with a dense shadow that moved into my thoughts. Without respite he sharpened my loneliness and impaled me with it. Then it was just a matter of time before I went mad.

There are many stories told in the town of Dunnville as to why I killed myself: that I had been cited for tax evasion or rum running, that I heard voices in the fields, that my brain went soft under the hot farmer's sun. What no one ever knew was that when I put the gun to my head I was trying to silence the voice shouting in my ear, the spirit Zulkanyan saying, 'Shoot, shoot.'

I am the Ghost of Garnet Warren. I came to the child Rachel Gold the same way Zulkanyan had come to me, in the fields of Knights Beach at Evans Point on the new moon in July 1968. I came the same wandering way but not with the same purpose. I found her out of longing not thirst. I didn't possess her. Rachel ignored her father's voice calling her home, which to her sounded like a droning crow, 'Raa. Raa.' What I heard was the name of my dead wife, Rachel. I followed until I found the girl by the lake, squatting in the sand dunes watching a mosquito suck blood into its belly. She sensed me right away. It was as if she were a spirit the way she knew I was there. She stood up and looked around, became impatient, slapped the mosquito drawing blood along her arm, then ran like hell.

# Book I

WHEN LIGHTNING FLASHED ACROSS THE SKY, Rachel Lynn Gold left the campfire and ran. She swept in circles down the field of her parents' farm until she reached the house at Knights Beach. Long shadows followed her in all directions. On the roof of the house the glass bulb of the lightning rod exploded. She kissed her father and mother goodnight and jumped under the covers just before the electricity cut out.

*Now I lay me down to sleep*
*I pray the Lord my soul to keep*
*And if I die before I wake*
*I pray the Lord my soul to take*

I watched her brush her teeth and followed her into her room, lay down beside her in the bed. I came quietly, trying not to thicken the air around her so she wouldn't be frightened. When I was close enough, I curled myself around her for warmth. I did this periodically every summer when Rachel was between the ages of seven and fourteen.

I bent over her sleeping body. Lay at the edge of the bed by her feet. I stood away from her when at thirteen she had nightmares and slept at the doorway to her sister Dana's room. The girl discovered my identity, one intuition following another: my book of accounts under the floorboards, the iron cauldron that I used for dying wool on the ceiling beams of the mud room at the back of the house, the photograph of me drinking with boxers in a Detroit speakeasy, my handwriting on the back: *me, Louis Kid Kaplan, Alex Borchuk and Al Capone*. The young Rachel pondered every detail of these things, building stories in her head.

She was right in believing that I loved water more than earth. I imagined the half a mile of lakefront as a picnic resort, added endless tons of sand we dug up from the dunes down the road that used to scale as high as mountain foothills right back from the waterline. I built a small shed near the large fence opening that surrounded the property on the south side of the road and when word spread, folks from Dunnville to Hamilton and Niagara Falls lined up on Sundays to pay one dollar a carload to come picnic on the beach and swim in the lake. Rachel's father was still using most of the fifty picnic tables I had built, for families to unwrap their peaches on, carve sausages and set out lemonade poured from thermos tumblers into Dixie paper cups. Of course, he had to load the picnic tables into the barn each year after Labour Day, repair loose or rotting boards and check for rusted protruding nails, making the tables ready for the first long weekend of the next summer, Victoria Day weekend. He drove my tractor. Didn't touch my rabbit traps. A city fellow in that way, he couldn't stand to see a suffering animal, would rather feed a bird sanctuary than let the local hunters shoot for game. The sight of a doe licking a blue salt block was Gold's idea of heaven, mine was hauling a bass into the boat. He didn't want to move me out and build some subdivision along the beach, and even though the land was his by deed, he erected dozens of houses on high poles with hundreds of little arched openings for purple martins to nest, believing it was his duty to respect the natural laws of the foxes, snakes, birds and trees. He praised the Indians who used to live here and spoke of me as a reluctant farmer and 'hospitality visionary' who was savvy enough to stash most of the gate cash in a tin box away from government taxes.

I haunted my own home. This made sense. I was beside Rachel when her fingers skimmed the pond silt for frogs, and when she brushed across the wheat fields waiting impatiently to grow taller than the feathers at the top of the stalks. I was there when she discovered she could smoke the hollow reeds that jet from the sand dunes.

When she heard from the boy at MacKay's corner store that I had buried all my money before I died and had left a note daring my second wife to find it, Rachel spent the next two days digging up to her knees behind the barn. Instead of treasure she found the shotgun I had used to kill myself.

I remember every detail of the day I died. I rose before the sun on God's day. Four or five mud wasps clicked their black bellies against the bedroom windows; there were hundreds more above in the rafters, swirling in darkness. Along the rim of the sills sleepy flies congregated, their eyes fixated on tiny spots of wallpaper.

I gave my dog the straight eye. 'Come, girl.' She dragged herself over the floor, sank her head into my lap at the edge of the bed. The oak bureau towered in front of us, its oval mirror faded by years of exposure to the turbulent lake air. Air saturated with dog dander and traces of manure from my hands. I twisted my hands together tightly before opening a drawer. An abundance of loose skin slid over my knuckles. Old boxer's knuckles, oversized and overused. They'd spent a lot of time in the leather of a cow's belly or beating on the leather of a man's face. Nothing personal, just one fight a week, years ago over in Detroit to make extra cash.

That day was a shaving day. I dressed in old jeans and a quarter-sleeve blue shirt, pulled on work boots with mud dried up to the ankles. Pungent well sulphur came up from the toilet as I relieved myself over the bowl filled with last night's urine. Cold water for a shave was good enough.

Outside sparrows rested like dozens of brown packages entwined along the telephone wires, beaks tucked down into their necks with crops full of seed. The morning was cold. In the fields, threads of white silk were bursting through the milkweeds. I didn't hear my footsteps crunching on the gravel road that ran straight down my property. I didn't hear anything that morning except my decision, which sounded like the heaviness a deaf man hears. My right shoulder where the butt of my shotgun rested ached all the way down to my fingers. The day before on my way to the lake I straddled the seat while reaching for the Remington pump strapped to the tractor's front fender, held the gun against the groove in my collarbone and pegged a black-billed duck out of formation. The salt pellet punched through the right wing; the duck's heart was vainly thrusting blood to the tips of the flight feathers when I snapped its neck.

The sound of the tractor never scared the birds, not even when I turned up fish skeletons with the rake, dragging the algae off the beach. It's silence that spooked them.

Sunday, September 2, 1960, I climbed to the top rafter of the barn behind my house and shot myself in the head. I fell over into the concrete trough where I used to keep feed for the cows. My spirit levitated through the roof of the barn... up, up. Out over the black walnut tree where the tent caterpillars had spun clouds into the branches, over the windmill I used for charging batteries, across to Sweets Corner where my brother lived, and up over the one-room schoolhouse where I met my second wife, Doris, at a Saturday social. While I was leaving this world, my two collies circled the barn howling like wolves. They chased their tails on their way to the house for help. My loyal Newfoundlander sat down at the trough and nuzzled her nose under my drooping arm.

And that was the end of Garnet in the flesh.

As I left my body I had heard ramblings of Zulkanyan's mother's kin, songs and sweet smells calling him back across the water. He glided the golden chain in the direction of these incantations, to the infant Kifli Talib. The *bomoh* was calling the priest Qadar to protect the sickly child of his line. The blood-drenched white goat's fur summoned like a neon marker.

I saw my death without the emotion I carried when clinging to the earthly plain. I was an observer who didn't care to be a middleweight boxer or a skilled bow hunter and bass fisherman.

Rachel spoke to me sometimes as if I were still alive. She had held dying things in her hand: Orville the mole and the seven rabbits. Peter Rabbit kicked in the ribs of Pink Bunny after Peter was accidentally fed poison-laced feed.

Rachel saw Pink Bunny take her last breath.

That whole summer Rachel contemplated death.

The ghost and the girl are rendered gracefully together. She has forgiven me for our second encounter when I swung the barn door shut, locking her in. She has also recovered from the heartbeats under the floorboards at the spot where my coffin had hung from the ceiling. That was Zulkanyan, reaching back along the golden chain, twisting his thin digits through the air on his way to Rachel's shoulder. Not the way he had approached me, snatching words out of my mouth or pushing thoughts into my head, which initiated a subtle depression, then anxiety and paranoia; with Rachel, the infrequent visitor was a Svengali whispering in her ear. So it did not surprise her a year later to be lifted out of bed in her sleep. 'Wake up,' her father said, cradling her in front of the television. 'A man is landing on the moon.'

*I will dream him up,*
*Yes, I will dream him up.*
*Then I will construct him*
*One piece at a time.*
    *RACHEL'S DIARY, 1975, AGE 14*

AT SEVENTEEN, at the time Rachel met Lynton, she forgot about me, became restless and disinterested as if I weren't there. She packed me up along with her childhood things. She lay next to Lynton on the floor of her room, reading Television lyrics from the back of an album cover. For the whole summer break they'd been driving in Lynton's red Mustang, lying around listening to Peter Gabriel and Bob Marley and Sly and Robbie and Jethro Tull and Johnny Winter and Humble Pie, getting stoned at house parties while listening to CFNY FM. That day was the same as the day before except when Rachel put the album cover down and smiled at Lynton, he sat up and kissed her.

He whispered 'I love you' down into the cave of her body. For the first time they spoke the language they were inventing. If Lynton had a needle he would have sewn Rachel's hands to his chest. This is what he imagined as he declared his love. As he closed his eyes.

He had waited all summer, he told her. He didn't expect anything. She hadn't thought of him in terms of love before, he was her friend. But now that it was done, it would never be any other way. The kiss was too strong. It drew her water toward him. It drew them together.

As they cast this love into their unworn hearts, their future unfurled for an instant. Then the whole of what was to come between them vanished, to be lived out in its own time.

Lynton took off, running face first into Rachel's bedroom door, as if all along he had planned to pass through it. 'I have to go.'

Her pink hands were sadly ripe for peeling him open. She tried to block his way, 'Say it again, say love,' but he had to leave to recapture what was left of his soul after giving himself away.

Lynton brought Rachel stones from his garden. Boxes of orange and chocolate Popsicles. He came to her with hair barrettes and coated elastics, a leather-bound copy of *The Lord of the Rings*, a delicate map of Middle Earth marking its rivers and lakes.

In the afternoons Rachel lay prostrate at Lynton's sleeping feet blowing hot breath on his soles and begging him to wake up and be with her after his night shifts at the Dofasco steel mill in Hamilton. Her hands hovered over his belly, measuring its rise and fall.

Consuming hash and cocaine, they made promises.

LYNTON LEANING OVER and kissing Rachel on the shady side of her grandmother's swinging kitchen door. Rachel looking down at the black-and-white diamond linoleum tiles, thinking Lynton is hers to possess. Her greatest pleasure is to weep with Lynton for their love and to hear, 'Oh God, Rachel.'

She couldn't have known she was setting herself up. *I give you my soul, Rachel Gold. Take it, please take it.* And she did. When Lynton said, 'Oh God, Rachel,' it pulled the water out of her like the moon tide, to him.

Maybe it was my fault. Maybe I had given her the impression that without someone to possess, the mortal world was monotonous. She gripped the seat of Lynton's jeans, pushing his hard zipper against her pubic bone, which seemed to be permanently, gloriously bruised. 'Let's go back to the car,' she said. 'Rachel,' he said in that way. Lynton cried her name like a wound, like a world, as if Rachel were the answer. She was a teenage girl. 'I love you, Lynton.' He stood back from her. Focused his eyes on hers. He brushed her hair back over her shoulders.

'I love you.'

'More than Heathcliff loves Catherine?'

'Oh God yes.'

'Do you love me as much as your dope?'

Silence.

'I don't love dope.'

'But you're always stoned.'

'I like it. There's nothing wrong with that, so do you.'

'I was just wondering if we could try and be straight for a couple of days.'

He put his lips to her mouth. 'I can't live without you.' He took her hand and pushed it to Nana's swinging kitchen door. Across the floor of diamonds they went, from the dark hall into a fusion of Nana's Russian Vaudevillian superstition and Uncle Joseph's residual Bombay fame.

Nana's silver tea server, which she used only for Passover and Hadassah meetings, sat on white linen that had been folded in half to fit the kitchen table. On a china plate, wedges of Nana's apple strudel and chocolate rugulah. Next to the plate was a glass dish full of Indian saffron milk fudge cakes from the Surati Sweet Mart. And Nana had on her high-heeled dancing shoes. Uncle Joseph had polished his head.

'Ta-dah,' Rachel sang. 'We're here. With news.' She took in the picture of the room. 'But first I have to say, I don't know what to do. I'm having an identity crisis.' She proceeded to flash one of her wide-faced smiles. 'If I don't eat Nana's strudel first, she'll be insulted, and if I leave Uncle Joseph's *kesri penda* waiting on the plate, which he knows is my favourite, I will seem like a traitor. My Indian blood is crying out for milk cake and my Yiddish ancestors are making bets up in heaven that I will side with them.'

She raised the back of her hand to her forehead, leaned to

one side and winked at Uncle Joseph, indicating the end of her performance.

Uncle Joseph jumped out of his chair. 'Bravo,' he said clapping. 'Bravo.'

Lynton rolled his eyes to the back of his head. 'You don't have Indian blood, Rachel.'

'Oh really? I have a grandmother who was adopted and there is family speculation that she was Indian.'

'Native Indian,' said Lynton. 'Not East Indian.'

'Bravo,' said Uncle Joseph. 'Bravo.' Then he belted out with perfect annunciation and pause:

*I give you the end of a golden string,*
*Only wind it into a ball:*
*It will lead you in at Heaven's gate,*
*Built in Jerusalem's wall.*

His performance was aimed at Nana who was pursing her lips and fluffing her hair. Rachel whispered into her grandmother's ear, 'I know for a fact, Nana, that the *mohantal* fudge cake over there is always served at weddings.'

'Oh my God, are you pregnant?' Nana said. 'Is that the news?'

'Guess what, everybody? Lynton's decided to be a poet.'

Nana did her fake smile, the really fake one that meant if Lynton had ever seemed eligible to marry her granddaughter, the pretense was over.

Uncle Joseph rose to his feet with great affect. 'Be warned,' he said. 'Becoming a poet may deepen your sadness. You are not happy with what you see, so you try to be like Timothy Leary. Misguided attempts.' Uncle Joseph didn't budge from below his hips but was swaying wildly from above. 'The slings and arrows of outrageous fortune are burning in you. What is it you want to say that has not been said before? The truth? But you are hiding, Lynton, in everything that distracts you from clarity.' Uncle Joseph bent down to kiss Lynton on his head. It was captivating. 'Now then,' he continued, 'if you still have to be a poet, try to preserve your health. Don't wreck yourself on the bud of passion—there lie the thorns.'

Lynton turned to Rachel. He raised his head and arched his shoulders back. 'Can we go now?'

At the end of the school year Rachel went to the formal with Lynton as her date. Lynton was two years older. He was in her sister Dana's class. She wore a turquoise taffeta dress with a ruffle in the back, an orchid on her wrist. Lynton in black leather and makeup. Later at a house party someone said Lynton had melted into a corner, dragging on a joint like a fag, ruining his perfect lipstick, his mascara running. He mumbled to Rachel that he was burning down. She took him home, a matador's purple blouse tucked into his thin waist. By the time they reached the unmade bed they were naked, made silent love. They didn't yet know there could be sounds for these feelings.

She hated him right after, she couldn't make him feel better no matter how much love she gave him. She knew as long as he came to her she would never refuse him. She wanted him to go. Then she wanted him to stay. It went on this way all through university. She told Lynton he was infected with the melancholy of the Romantic poets and she couldn't help; she was infected too. 'We don't do anything,' she said. 'I know nothing makes sense. Don't you think I know that? If you keep bringing yourself to me, I'll keep having you.'

At dawn Lynton left her one of his notes and went to the lake. He was at least a mile out when the storm came, bringing five-foot waves of green darkness. Having lost the fibreglass body of the two-man boat, he clung to the sail. He was picked up some hours later by the crew of a ship that was drilling for oil on the point. Lynton walked back to Rachel in a diagonal across the lawn. Topless. Hypothermic. 'I told you about the storms on the lake,' she said. 'Drowning is the worst ending.'

He took off his shorts and folded his arms around his chest. He stood by her bed shivering cold and crying but he wasn't going to beg her to comfort him. She let him turn purple while she thrashed around the bed in anguish, then she lifted the covers and plucked the algae out of his long, straight hair.

WHEN RACHEL FOUND A LETTER from Lynton to her older sister, Dana, she broke. After years of loving him. After Lynton followed the Grateful Dead to New York and Denver and wherever they toured that summer, and came home and wouldn't shave or eat or wash himself; after he swallowed a ton of pills and a glass of whisky and locked himself in his hotel room, hoping to die; after he returned from India, when he was spiritual. Lynton still having to survive a drug trial. At the same time that Rachel realized she was still in love with him, she found the letter, which had been lying under the bathroom sink for at least a year.

When Rachel read the letter, she went into shock and lost her voice, and it was all very sudden. She would have preferred if it had been slower, like the fragility she had felt when she didn't see Lynton at school morning prayers or when she was alone listening to the radio. All of a sudden she became a broken thing. In an instant she was finished. She was silenced. Nothing could help her. That she had the rest of her life only made it worse. She swore she was dead.

Lynton had written to Dana from the same pen he had inked Rachel love. The same ink. The same water. He didn't mention Rachel at all. He must have been possessed. He wrote Dana's name, which didn't belong to him. Dana belonged to Rachel. Lynton belonged to Rachel. After reading the letter, she was thinner than the fibres of the page and smaller than a dot over an *i*. She was nothing at all.

Rachel had only read *Dear Dana* when she broke. The moaning and howling came later.

How could he be someone else behind her back, to her own sister who was colder than the coldest diamond, nastier than the meanest mask? Dana, who hadn't even read Kafka or Plath, who had stinky feet and bitten fingernails.

The only thing that Rachel knew then was that she would never speak again. Her body screeched and collapsed inside.

SHE IS IN HER LIVING ROOM at noon. The weather is good.

At twenty-three, she is too young to look back very far
has come to no conclusions—no fear of finality. There is fear
The kind before regret. She is not closed—has no idea wha
it is to become that way.

She approaches a bookcase. Books burden her; she can'
leave a room unless she has handled them. She must at leas
read the titles. This is her obsession, the nature of paper, th
ink sinking into the page, how deeply embedded, how long o
short the words. Sentences should run the length of a breath
The words should flow to the extent of the air in her lungs
Until she lost her voice she read everything out loud, ignoring her poor pronunciation of characters' names. Often she
makes up what she expects to read next.

It is 1984, the year the world can no longer ignore the
African starvation. Indira Ghandi is murdered, AIDS is offi-
cially pronounced, USA goes into debt, Greenpeace *Rainbou
Warrior* is blown up by the French army. Two fat pigeons si
poised on Rachel's bed in the early afternoon. She doesn'
know how they entered her apartment, twenty-four floors up
She never opens the windows.

When Rachel walks into the room undressing for her bath, she discovers them. Maybe they flew in to cool off, but Rachel thinks they walked in, one Cro-Magnon claw in front of the other, step by step in silence. One is preening, its head swung under its wing, a headless bird.

Pigeons are familiar to her from above, but there below on the bed they are inflated, grey and reverent.

Rachel often flies in dreams. Sometimes she floats across the woods in her parents' yard, through the bark of the maple tree into the sap and out the spout of the tapped tree, more watery than the rain. She lifts off the ground like a Harrier Jet, suspending herself over the woods. Looking for Lynton, who she loves.

In the bath Rachel sinks under the running faucet. She sponges along the fullness of her breastbone, where her white meat is.

She sings to the birds, 'Sisters of Mercy,' in harmony with Leonard Cohen's voice coming across a scratchy record. Singing for the first time since she gave up her voice. So the first sounds are soft but big, peeping out of her mouth, shaking her insides. That she can make the sound come out, now after three months of talking only in her dreams. She leads the pigeons to the balcony, where they look out at the sky and fly away.

The next morning Rachel rolls out of her bed. In the exact spot where she had placed her feet the night before there is an egg. Her hands fumble for it. She puts the egg next to her ear in case it is ticking. There could already be a heartbeat— wings blooming. She warms her hands with hot water in the kitchen sink. The egg fits perfectly into Rachel's fist as she transports it to her grandmother's house.

'It wasn't there yesterday,' she tells Nana, giving her the egg without asking what her grandmother will do with it.

'Now that you can sing,' Nana says, 'you're no longer unreachable. You can forgive.'

Nana has ten one-hundred-dollar bills folded in her change purse, 'For an emergency.'

'I don't need it.'

'What am I going to do with it? Will you write?'

'Always, always, my postcards. Uncle Joseph's India will heal me. Just like the foxtrot makes you feel young.'

'I'm not so old, Rachel. It's my bones that deceive.'

'I can fly around the world collecting adventures the way you collect dance trophies. Ladies and gentlemen, introducing Smooth Moves Nana Gold of Miami Beach at the Beau Rivage Hotel on Collins Avenue, just down the street from Wolfies, with her dancing partner, the man of the evening, Mr. Heartburn so-and-so, formerly from the Catskills.'

'Mr. Heartburn had quite a two-step.' Nana shakes her head. 'Don't hate your sister, Rachel.'

'I do, I wish she was dead.'

'Try not to.'

Rachel began to cry.

'What about him?'

Silence.

'You might not always love Lynton, but Dana will always be—'

'I can't help it.'

'Take the money.'

'I have to see what's out there, Nana. Uncle Joseph said so. He said if I want to know who I am, I have to be in the world. I need to learn about what's inside of me. I can't just stay here. I have a round-the-world ticket. Look at all these places, Nana. I wish you could come. I'll send your love to Uncle Joseph.' Rachel held her grandmother's narrow chin in her hands. She kissed Nana's eyelids, knowing she had memorized the ancestral eyes underneath. And the smell of her grandmother's still perfectly soft, petal skin had permanently pressed into Rachel, long before she ever knew Nana wouldn't be there forever.

**Tel Aviv, Israel**
On a postcard of the Dome of the Rock:

*Nana,*
*Maybe I know how you felt when you came here after Grandpa died. Isn't this where we get saved?*
*I put a note in The Wall. It was for you. Rachel*

**Cairo, Egypt**
On a postcard of a full moon behind the Great Pyramid of Pharaoh Khufu at Giza:

*Nana,*
*At the Pink Sphinx Disco you have to check your gun.*
*Hitched a ride to the Pyramids but had to listen to John Denver all the way there. I kept asking our guide (whose English I barely understood) who built the pyramids. He said criminals, workers, slaves and whatever. So I asked again if it was the Jews. He said he had no information to confirm that. After noon, even with the air conditioning, all I want to do is sleep. Did you know you can see a heat wave?*

**Lausanne, Switzerland**
On a postcard of Lake Ouchy:

> *The last line in Lawrence Durrell's novel Clea—*
> *Vision is exorcism.*

**Rome, Italy**

> *Dear Nana,*
> *I met Mom and Dad and Dana at the La Residenza Hotel.*
> *Why did I agree to this? If Dana comes near me, I'll kill her.*
> *Love you*
> *Rachel*

**New Delhi, India**
On a postcard of the Taj Mahal:

> *Nana,*
> *Uncle Joseph called us to India from his grave. For no other reason, it seems, than to have one of his big-bellied laughs.*

INDIA WAS UNCLE JOSEPH'S CREATION. Uncle Joseph, Indian screen star and long-time designated extra family member. Mr. Gold brought Uncle Joseph home from work one evening after selling him a brand-new bungalow on a corner lot. 'Jewish Indian,' their father said. 'Indian Jew. Very religious.' Rachel thought of Uncle Joseph as the only person who was really alive at all. He brought India into their house, under a brown bald head and reams of lines from Tagore and Shakespeare—off by heart and in a more elegant accent than the British. Uncle Joseph clapped for more, more, bravo, when Rachel did her Flip Wilson as Geraldine impersonation. She put her hands on her hips and shook her bright face like a sunflower. 'You're going to be a great woman of the stage,' he said.

To Rachel India was a little red bean from Uncle Joseph that had an ivory elephant for a lid. Inside the bean were one hundred elephants carved from ivory. Two beans. One for Rachel and one for Dana. They had to use a magnifying glass to see the one hundred little elephant trunks. Rachel counted. 'The carver soon went blind,' Uncle Joseph said. 'Only so many elephants before an eye wears out.'

India was a black silk scarf with real gold thread. The most colourful place in the world. Indigo silk, ruby red jewels, gold swords and orange spices, which turned everything in the pot orange.

Uncle Joseph didn't lie about India. He saw what he wanted to. What he could see. Its fine qualities. That's because he saw people's spirit instead of their fleshes. He saw what floated around on waves.

India wasn't like the elephant bean at all or anything like the old black-and-white movies. It was starving like Lynton's India, with a few creamy characters whom Rachel referred to as the bedecked and bejewelled.

Fortunately, the night they landed in India the Golds met Lennart the Swede who was also taxied to the wrong terminal and missed the connecting flight to Delhi. Huddling together at the airport, tired and ill-tempered, they watched the untouchables sweeping litter into filthy concrete corners.

Apparently, according to the suspicious customs officials, the Gold family had never entered India. They had snuck in somehow without getting their passports stamped. So without the entrance stamp, of course, they could not get an exit stamp when they wanted to leave. As it was put, 'You are not here, and therefore, you cannot go.' It was Lennart the Swede who realized the potential influence of Uncle Joseph and relayed the close relationship of the Gold family to the film star and how they had come to visit his gravestone and how they must be here because there is flesh and bone in front of the magistrate, even if the passports had been overlooked during the unfortunate mishap when they were all—including himself, a seasoned traveller, who did get his passport stamped by some fluke, but could have easily missed the occasion himself—sent to the wrong terminal by the Air India contact. 'So, please, find the bloody stamp. Have the official compassion to help this grieving family.'

After some lengthy forms were filled out and rupees handed over, the customs official stamped passports and personally escorted the Gold family and Lennart to another terminal, where they caught the last plane to Delhi.

Rachel sat beside Lennart on the way and exclaimed that her meal was the best aeroplane food she had ever had in her life. She thought they'd be stuck in that airport forever and now they were off the ground in their own little universe. 'Isn't this relaxing? I hope we never land.' The Swede ingratiated himself with the Gold family not only by his heroic gesture with the customs official and, all things being relative, his vast knowledge of the ways of India, but also because he was looking quite lost and dishevelled. His cold blue eyes were pleading to join in. Lennart deftly avoided the disdain Rachel and Dana had for one another by speaking to one sister at a time and conducting the conversation with civil formality. He accompanied the family from the airport to their hotel, making arrangements to meet them for breakfast the next morning, and was promptly invited to come with them on their tour of Red Fort, which to everyone's amazement, Lennart declined. Instead, he enthusiastically accepted an invitation to dinner the next evening.

Lennart, unusually brooding for a Swede in summer, became the family mascot, counselling the Golds on issues of concern. He advised not to take tea in their room because it would inevitably arrive cold, and don't expect you can fully communicate to your driver, better bring him into the hotel every morning to go over the plans for the day with a hotel representative, do not change the plans once they are made, it will take at least another day to recover from the ensuing chaos. Always carry bottled water and use it for everything, tooth brushing and cleaning cuts and scrapes, even washing your hands, girls, do not smile at men, cover up in holy places, lines move slowly, it can take a whole day for instance to get stamps at the post office, pay a bit more and get them at the hotel, if, however, you are stuck in a line, take turns waiting while the others rest on a ledge or a flight of stairs, never pay asking price, if you give a beggar money it doesn't mean he'll go away, he might even bring friends. There is no shame in squatting over a toilet, hold your nose and breathe through your mouth, but remember to lock your teeth together so flies don't sail down your throat. I can find you good silks and gold. I will not deal in ivory.

In Rachel and Dana's room Lennart was staring at himself sideways in the mirror seemingly in disbelief at the image reflecting back at him. Sallow thin lips, eyes set in a purple dugout. 'You must eventually love India. It is your duty to your uncle and besides, the only reason why you don't love India is because you're planning to leave her too soon, before you have the chance to fall in love.' He was still looking at himself, thinking, How do lips get so pale? That's probably a bad sign.

'I have to keep moving,' said Rachel. 'I'll know it when I find it. Right, Lennart?'

Dana sighed noisily and clicked her tongue against her teeth. She was tempted to say something to her sister like, 'You've never known anything,' or 'You're pathetic, Rachel. No wonder...' That would be enough. Dana and Rachel didn't have to finish sentences.

THEY HAD BEEN TO THE TAJ MAHAL and Red Fort, to Gandhi's house and the eternal flame of his burial site, where Rachel removed her flimsy shoes and set them down beside hundreds of other flimsy shoes and slippers. She approached the flame with a tickle in her heart, holding back tears like one fends off a sneeze. Rachel suspected she had picked up the sadness of the multitudes through the smooth stone sanded down by the shuffle of bare feet.

Now they had flown to Bombay for a few days to find Uncle Joseph. Much of the city ran over them in the crushing heat making them moody and panicked; beggars rushed around the motorcar in swarms and stuck out their arms like haunted branches, waving for rupees. Dana and Rachel held silk scarves soaked with jasmine oil under their noses to filter out the stench. Mr. Gold was up with the driver negotiating the terms for driving services for the next few days, trying to keep his mind away from his asthma, to keep the girls from finding out how sick the air made him. The three women were in the back. They stopped at a light and a flurry of hands shot into the cab.

'Roll it up faster, Rachel,' Dana said to her sister, who was so rushed to turn the black handle of the window she pulled it slightly off its screw.

'If you think you can do it better,' Rachel said, 'you sit on the end. Why do you always get the middle?'

'Mom,' Dana said, 'roll up your window.' She nudged her mother. 'Roll it up.'

It was a long traffic light. Time slowed down—stretched out. Dana slapped one of the branch arms to get it out of the way for the window. A long thin grubby arm that didn't extend from its shoulder, but unhinged from its elbow like a moat bridge. Dana reached over Rachel and grabbed the handle.

'Get off me,' Rachel said. 'I'll do it.'

Dana shoved her hand into Rachel's lap.

'What are you doing?' Rachel said.

'My scarf. I dropped it. Where is it?'

'I don't know. How should I know?'

Dana pulled Rachel's blue scarf away from her and held it to her nose.

'Hey,' Rachel said. She elbowed Dana in the ribs. Hard, like she was getting her for the whole thing. 'Give it back.'

They both saw Dana's green scarf on the floor. Rachel reached down to pick it up. There was the blue-green of twisted silk and yellow-brown of jasmine oil and heavy festering air, both heads bent down and when they straightened back up to the window, he was there. His veil had fallen, so every detail of his thin face filled the window space.

His nose was where his ear should have been, which was at the back of his head somewhere, if he had an ear at all. His mouth, where his cheek would have been, was a thin crust of contorted flesh over which he had little control.

He was a ghost for sure, he was a walking horror, and the fright he created by his sudden appearance rose out of their mouths, all the way up from their toes. 'Ahhh. Ahhh.'

He saw how he shocked them. In slowtime, he looked into the eyes of Rachel, Dana and Mrs. Gold and saw their woeful hearts. He was used to disgust. Disgust was how he elicited pity and rupees. They hadn't seen him coming, so there wasn't time for disgust. It was all contemptuous lament and tears. With his eyes, which were half in the right place, the beggar gave the women a wide bloodshot look that apologized for the violence of his face. He had only meant to elicit charity, not fear, not that kind of repulsion.

He quickly pulled his hand in from the window and reset his veil, looked to the ground and slipped away.

Mrs. Gold was the first to recover. She felt great pity as soon as the shock moved over. This reflexive compassion was her value, it made up for so many things she didn't possess: for her lack of metaphor, and her naïveté, and her depression. It was why they all loved her and why they couldn't be like her. Mrs. Gold had great compassion for any homeless or motherless creature as long as they were homeless or motherless, which Rachel and Dana were not.

'Poor soul,' she said. 'We took his dignity away.'

The girls were sobbing. Rachel covered her face blue. Dana covered her face green. The light changed and the motorcar went on.

The one thing they had all agreed to was a pilgrimage to Uncle Joseph's grave. It was as if he alone could join them together, somewhat reluctantly, for a mission of the heart. Because they all loved him. And he, too, loved them, just the way they were. He had mentioned to Nana, only three days before he took ill, that India had always been good to the Jews. And for his family remaining there, and for others, some of whom had been known to follow Uncle down the street singing his praises, he would return to the home that made him feel welcome his whole life. Just the way he was.

They got out of the motorcar at the railway station and made their way to the cemetery on foot. It seemed like an eternity, past the Mahalaxmi racecourse and the *dhobi ghat*. One hundred or so hand laundry stalls where cotton was beaten on stone. 'I'll just wait here at the track,' Dana said. 'I don't need to see a grave.' No one even bothered to reply. Then Rachel said, 'Let her go. Then we never have to see her again.' Past the Muslim cemetery and the Hindu cremation site, having no idea, when they finally made it to the gates with the Star of David, how they were going to find their beloved uncle.

A decision was made for everyone to split up and investigate. They wandered around like mice in a maze, or big fat Indian rats weaving between Indian marble.

Uncle Joseph hadn't died down. He simply died. And not the greatest performance of his life. He wasn't feeling very well at the time. His brief decline was not reminiscent of his passions or his movies. Not anywhere close to the man that kept Nana in a constant state of baking and shopping for nylon stockings and stylish shoes. A man who gracefully retired from the film lots of Bombay to Nana's almost breeze-less backyard.

'Hey,' said Dana, 'let's go. We're not going to find him.' Mr. and Mrs. Gold agreed. They filed out and washed their hands. Rachel was distraught that they had come all that way and she wasn't able to leave her love at Uncle's bones. A gathering of squatters who lived outside the gate had come to beg. 'Okay,' she said. 'Okay, everyone,' she shouted to the crowd. 'Uncle would have wanted me to tell you that it is never too late to change your lot in this world. And I am also telling you that you are all very lucky to be so close to the resting place of such a great man. Uncle Joseph,' Rachel cried, 'man to man is so unjust. You don't know who to trust. Your worst enemy could be your best friend. And your best friend your worst enemy. And furthermore,' she continued, 'who the cap fit let them wear it.' She bowed. With her hands before her heart, paying homage to the light in all living things. '*Namaste*.' She pulled whatever money she had out of her pocket and handed it about. Mr. and Mrs. Gold followed her out of the cemetery. 'Come on, Dana, let's go,' she said.

The Golds flew Air India through Amritsar on the day the Golden Temple was bombed. They had to wait on the tarmac to identify their luggage, were made to stand next to the aeroplane until every piece was accounted for. They were on their way to Kashmir to calm down from the city. It took twice as long as they had planned to get there. By that time, twice as long seemed fast. Indian time was slowtime, which sometimes translated into the feeling that they were somewhere other than on the planet Earth—perhaps in a dream.

When the Golds tumbled out of the car at the dock on their way to Dahl Lake, Mr. Gold had to count their luggage again. This time, they thought, he was counting so no one would steal their suitcases, but it was only for the boatmen to figure out how many *shikara* taxi boats were needed to take them to their houseboat.

The man who helped Rachel into the *shikara* had a crescent moon tattooed on his hand where a pencil would rest. She looked at the blue ink and then covered it with the grip of a handshake. He shook her off as soon as she was steady in the boat. The picture: Rachel lying on her back in the gondola-style taxi, a floating bed named *Pin Up Girl*.

They were taxied to their rented houseboat where they met two brothers, Nizme (handsome) and Ahmed (dismissive), and their blind father who took the rent money for the floating palace and disappeared. The Golds dispersed throughout the houseboat, claiming bedrooms and reading books from the wood-panelled library, which housed Gordon Sinclair's *Footloose in India* and *In Search of Secret India* by Paul Brunton, which Rachel had already read. Dana took *Birds of Kashmir* and *Beautiful Valleys of Kashmir and Ladakh, etc.etc*, into the huge living room, stretched out on a red velvet couch, and raised her feet on a few brightly coloured silk pillows. Nizme, the younger brother, stood at the ready with bottled water in his hand. He stood like a statue at the edge of the Kashmiri rug. Whenever a *shikara* paddled by, a soft current pushed into the houseboat, giving everyone the feeling they were drifting out to sea, and causing the dining-room chandelier to tinkle.

What could be more revealing than to watch them all together? How fortunate no one from home was there to see the four of them lying in a *shikara*—as if in their graves. Soon the weather would be stuck to them all. They would be stuck to each other.

Nizme took his place at the back. 'Nishat Garden,' he pointed across the lake. 'Over there.' He heaved his breath over his knees as he paddled the heart-shaped oar, eyes fixed on the tiny island.

Rachel watched him. She adjusted her skirt down over her ankles. She counted his strides to twenty and then back to the beginning, found a way to get his attention by whispering his name into the air just before the beginning of each stroke. 'Nizme,' into the water and along. 'Nizme,' into the water and along. Nizme...Nizme...He looked up from the water to the sky, squinted, looked down from the thick clouds pasted onto the roof of the day, smiled at her. 'Nizme,' into the water and along. 'How come *you* always have to row? What's wrong with your brother?'

Mrs. Gold made a face that Rachel assessed as rabid, so she held up her hands to deflect the image. 'Do you mind, Mom? I'm talking to Nizme, not you.'

'He can't hear you back there,' Dana said. 'He can't hear a word you're saying.'

At the dock a boy squatted in a fern, peering out at Rachel from the camouflage. Black eyes on a brown face. 'What kind of garden is this? I don't see any flowers,' she said.

'Soon,' said Nizme. 'It's not time for the bloom.' He opened his arms as if they were a doorway to step through into the Nishat garden. He would wait by the *shikara* and smoke.

The boy from the fern followed the sisters when they took off from their parents. He crossed in front of them and puffed out his chest. He was a Hindu in a Muslim sea. His *dhoti* pants twisted around his belly button. Rachel rested her eyes there. He called her over to a line of chinar trees. 'Smell, behind here, jasmine.'

Dana turned up her nose. She wasn't getting any lavish niceties from the skinny marionette. She told him he was just another little beggar hiding in the woods; she waved at the big-eyed bug with her hand as if to say, 'Shoo, shoo.'

'My name,' he said puffing himself up a little more, 'is Nobody.' He took Rachel's hand and led her to the bark of a cypress. As she leaned in to take a breath of its silver skin, Nobody nudged his face close to her ear. 'I love you.'

'Pardon?'

'*Je t'aime*,' he said. 'I love you.'

'Ha, you're only a child.'

'I am sixteen.'

'I say you are twelve.'

Rachel noted a clearing of soft grass. Two bodies could lie there in the tangled wood. It would be a good place to rest. To hide. Forever.

In the Nishat garden Nobody was his own man. He knew every inch of path and where natural breaks made ways through the fruit trees and lilac thickets. He always wanted money and wanted to get it without asking like a beggar. Instead he would ask for a piece of candy, a pen, or a shoelace. He might point to a T-shirt and shrug as if he knew it was a crazy idea to take the shirt off a back, but this is a crazy world and in the Mougal garden a foreign T-shirt could have value and prestige.

Nobody chose Rachel. Dana hadn't even noticed him in the ferns when the *shikara* landed. Rachel thought he knew she was broken, and that Dana was guilty of murdering her heart.

He put his beggar-boy joy around Rachel. A kind of light that solicited generosity. She happily gave him two rupees before stepping out of his world. He would make a killing, she thought, if he played an instrument.

Rachel and Dana walked up then down the terraces, coming around to the sight of their parents on a grassy hill. 'Go on if you want to,' their father said. He rolled his eyes when he saw his daughters. On a flat spread of soft grass, before all to see, just above the lowest slopes that were used as latrines, Mrs. Gold was parading around in a red costume that had been pinned down her back. Strands of tarnished silver chains hung around her neck and a headdress with the same dull metal fringe had transformed her into a Kashmiri doll. Rouge had been smeared across her cheeks. Two squatted and toothless men were showing her, by example, how to coyly turn her head for the perfect photo that they would then sell to her at a premium.

Rachel ran back to the threshold of the wild garden. She held up a ten-rupee note for Nobody to see, rolled it tightly and placed it into the ground.

There were little patches of shrubbery in Rachel's history. As a child, standing under the maple trees, sifting through the raspberry bushes at Upper Wellington and Irving Crescent (named after her grandfather Irving Gold), a summer day with red seeds in her mouth, being herself a seedling, she had grown roots. Each time her father purchased more land, she was pulled further to the ground. Land was heavy and deeds were official with red wax seals and sometimes a ribbon. Walking through her father's fields was rather like carrying

Russian novels on her back, which translated into a pond, a ghetto of apartment buildings, a two-hundred-year-old oak tree and a canoe to paddle down the man-made lake that used to be her summer camp.

One summer a tractor had slid into the lake. While Rachel stood guard at the edge of the mudslide waiting for her father, she heard a freckled boy say, 'Let Gold buy a new tractor. He can afford it. Let it sink.' Rachel listened as other kids joined in about her father and the stinking rich and some older teenagers saying, 'All the fucking Jews are cheap bastards.' She was the owner's daughter hiding behind an ice cream sandwich.

It wasn't the first time, but after that incident Rachel kept separate from what she called the GP (general public). They frightened her, as did her schoolteachers, who expected the regurgitation of misleading, inaccurate materials. And the redneck police. In the next war she wanted to stand on her front lawn and blow their heads off before they came after her. But probably, she knew, she would hide in the cellar with the Ghost of Garnet Warren.

Human recklessness imposed an ugly style that she rebelled against by washing herself into thin pieces of light and dispersing them into those she loved. And her father she loved most of all. She would shine her pieces on him whenever he was caving in. Rachel had so much light that she thought there was enough for everyone. Yet when Lynton touched her, he gripped onto her bones and still it wasn't enough to make him want to be whole.

At the houseboat, on a postcard of the Vatican, she wrote, *A boy named Nobody loves me*, and sent it to Nana.

The next day the electricity failed.

Rachel climbed the ladder to the roof of the houseboat. Up there she could see the colourful *shikaras* sprinting through the water and the white hats on the rowers' heads looking grey-blue in the dim day. A dozen naked boys were swimming at the far shore. When they kicked their feet up Rachel saw streamers, pink like sand, moving across the water.

After a while, the tail of her loneliness wrapped itself around her. In the corner of her sight Dana's head emerged from the deck below, then her body rose in increments like an unwanted apparition in slowtime. Rachel observed her sister scrupulously, with a fog in front of her that her Chinese doctor years later would diagnose as a web of mucus around her heart. Dana was rundown from the sweltering watery heat, from being stung by the touch of too many beggars.

Rachel took a deep breath, as people do when they arrive in the countryside expecting something clean. The air was full of monsoon water. Smelly and hanging low. Rotting garbage and sewage seized her lungs squeezing without relief. Clinging to her hair and the wooden pores of the houseboat and the white hats on the lake. There was no wind.

The putrid air settled in the food. It overcame the curry and the coriander and stirred itself into Rachel's dreams. The only thing it didn't penetrate was Dana's hair. Rubbed with patchouli oil, Dana's hair was the best smell for miles. Rachel was tempted to bury her face in it to find relief. Instead, she stood beside her sister wishing Dana was dead—and not so beautiful.

On the other side the splashing boys became a blur of pink. Rachel felt her sweaty, fleshy thighs rubbing against her cotton pants. When Dana moved next to her, she turned and said, 'Why are you always following me?' Dana didn't answer. Rachel looked back across the lake and said, 'I wonder if they like swimming in shit.'

'They were born in it. We just make it.'

'They seem happier than us.'

'That wouldn't be hard.'

Rachel thought of herself as a dead body in need of burning. Something jumped up and down in the sunken space between her breasts. She wished it would fly away. It was a long time before she said, 'How long do you think those boys will live, swimming in sewer water? They have to get sick sometime, don't they?' She pointed a pink finger to the other side. 'I bet tomorrow they'll be carving cricket bats in a suffocating room.'

'I hate having servants,' Dana said. 'They're not even good ones.'

'Oh, then it's bad servants you can't stand.'

Dana didn't answer. She wore a frown that made her face look black. Black kohl ran under her eyes. Finally she said, 'I wish I never came.'

'Why did you? Why didn't you stay home with Lynton?'

'Who?'

'My boyfriend.'

'Fuck off, Rachel.'

'Well, did you?'

'None of your fucking business. You didn't even want him anymore.'

'It's that simple to you, isn't it? As if you know what happened. As if you get it, right, Dana? Can't you find your own fucking life? Do you have to take everything of mine?'

Rachel and Dana folded their arms across their chests and squeezed, both of them insular, in the margins of despair.

'I don't have a sister,' Rachel said.

'I don't have one either.'

'Fine.'

The giggling boys splashed on the other side.

'Just say you did it, Dana.'

'Forget about him. I don't care about him.'

'Just say it.'

'I don't care about you either, Rachel.'

The rain had been falling quietly over the white hats in the *shikara*s and onto the boys in the water making them laugh louder than chimes, arms and legs slapping all over. Then the rain came down harder and the boys still played but the sound was taken out of them—out of the world. It was the same as when Rachel lost her voice, except now the silence had moved from her mouth up into her ears.

The air was a flame.

The sky seemed very close to the lake. There wasn't much space between the top of the world and its floor. An infinity of intimacy exists in this kind of weather. Rachel remembered Lynton's cheeks, his hands, the parts of him she loves the most. She pictured his salient hands all up inside her, and her resting on his hip bones, which stuck out like girls' hips.

Dana's stomach was sour, her mouth was hot, her head and neck burned. Signs of vulnerability to the weather and to the stupid people, including her parents, who didn't understand what she was trying to say when she threw up over the side of the *shikara* on the way home from Nishat Garden.

For three days she emptied her body into the toilet and over her bed, puked across the floor on the way to the bathroom, crawled wherever she went. She would have cried if she had the energy but there wasn't enough water left in her.

Nizme stood at the door with bottles of water. Mr. and Mrs. Gold scurried in and out of the room saying words like, 'Delhi belly?' or 'Dysentery?' or 'Malaria?' Sometimes they said the words as a firm diagnosis. 'Delhi belly, Dana.' Then, 'It's not malaria, you'd be much sicker.' Then, 'Dysentery symptoms like in the book. We'd better get a doctor.'

Rachel stayed away from her sister's illness. She went to the Congo with Conrad instead. When she finished there she went to Malaysia as a preacher with Maugham. All the while she was reading she could hear Dana begging their parents to take her home.

She was too sick. How would they move her?

Finally, after three days, Rachel went to Dana's room. For all Rachel knew Dana was dying. If this was Dana's punishment it had gone on long enough. The room stank like the slums of Calcutta. Dana had slithered down the side of the bed and was hanging over a pail. The covers were thrown into a heap on the floor. She wouldn't remember that Rachel had come. She would only remember Nizme carrying her to the *shikara* at dusk and paddling out on the lake for the breeze to bring her fever down in the din of the Muslim call to prayer. Voices that came out of the mountains. Dana was burning in a different way than Rachel. Rachel could be burning for years, if Dana couldn't hold water soon, she would burn out.

Dana remembered Rachel saying Lynton had a drug contact in these foothills. Lynton could have walked along Polo View Road like her and Rachel. A kilo of hash was nothing to the Kashmiri trade, but to Lynton's stomach...Maybe Dana was hallucinating, but in fact she was remembering two days earlier, when papaya was pulped into juice and Dana and Rachel drank it while walking down a dead-end street where men were shitting on slabs of concrete, dozens of them with their pyjama shirts up. Uncle Joseph had never mentioned this kind of thing. How could he not have known? Someone grabbed her. Who? I don't know, I didn't see. Keep walking. Then Rachel was bitten by a hand too. They kept coming. One violation after another. 'Vandals,' Rachel yelled. 'Which one of you did it?' There were swarms of men lifting their pyjama shirts.

Rachel became a bull, kicking the dust in a circle around Dana. Who touched my sister? Shameless cowards, come here so I can kill you. No one understood her words, they understood her animal sounds and her body talk. They laughed. Rachel saw a man reaching out. She said it was like slow motion once she had an eye on it. She caught his arm with a victory shout. She was going to snap it off, break it, the thin little bugger. Yet, once she had savoured the idea of maiming him, she was satisfied and let him go. 'Run, Dana, run.'

'How are you?'

'What?'

'I think we should send for a doctor.'

'I wouldn't let one of them touch me—never.'

Black bile came up into the pail. Dana shat her bed.

Before this, Rachel had wished for her sister to die. Dana was guilty of lying and breaking and stealing. Treason. Dismissing love and bending it. Wearing it as if she didn't care about it.

Now, Rachel raises Dana's arm and strokes under it with a cool wet cloth—the way Jews do when they wash their dead, without turning the stiff limb, lifting it straight up instead. She knows that karma is a cycle and assumes Dana is experiencing hers. Life repeats itself like a printed cloth.

Without an apology she tries to forgive Dana in absentia.

It's too soon.

She lifts Dana's arm and holds the weight of it, the dead weight that is tired from being attached to a purged body, from being a leg to walk on instead of her real legs, which won't work. Legs that have excused themselves and gone to sleep.

So the arm is heavy. The body empty like a martyr.

It just happened. Not because Dana was a thief and a traitor. She ate popcorn from a cart on the street in Delhi. A mountain of white, pure and clean in the middle of an infested street. They had all laughed at the absurd sight, as out of place as it would be to see a leper on Bloor Street in Toronto. When Dana ate the popcorn, she wished she were in a cool dark movie house.

It was clean and white and hid a disease that took fifty hours to make her retch. First it landed on her cells like a lunar module. Dana's sickness wasn't a punishment, it was bad judgment. She ate dirty from a clean hand.

Rachel would have been sick too, except she was shooing flies away from the ankle she scraped while getting out of the car. Dozens of flies found her in seconds, came to dip their swords in her blood. They found the scrape before Rachel knew she had it. Rachel said popcorn was out of place in India, too contrived. She kept saying, 'Why don't you give up and eat Indian food? Potato curry won't kill you. Masala dosa is good for breakfast. Just don't order food that doesn't belong here.' Rachel's illness would come later. It was waiting for her in her sleep. She held the dead weight of her sister's hand. 'For God's sake, Dad, go get a doctor.'

She went to Dana's feet and held them as if her hands were shoes. 'Take her out of this sick room, Nizme, to the lake, but don't let her touch the water; she has enough parasites. You can't let her die when I hate her so much. Where's the doctor? It's just phlegm coming out of her now. She's down to losing her own blood. She smells like shit. Take her to the water; it's an oven in here. She's not shivering now, she's sweating. She's light. You can carry her. Watch her feet, they want to be protected—there's a map of her body written on the bottom. Her feet need air. They need to be suspended, over a pillow or over your knees. Go into the lake with her, Nizme, go under the prayers from the hills, in the breeze.'

Then Rachel was alone in the diseased room, full of Dana's lies, full of her confusion and uncertainty. Dana lingered on the sick-smelling sheets in Rachel's hands. Rachel didn't want to know about it. She wasn't ready to see that what had killed her heart was also a desperate thing.

The young Indian doctor carried a black bag. It reminded Rachel of the ones doctors used to carry when they went to visit women who were dying of boredom. A black bag, which contained a pharmacy. He said dysentery, right away. Throwing up, diarrhoea, no food or water to keep. 'Yes,' he said, 'yes, yes.' He shook his head. Not the way the street Indians did when Rachel asked for directions, 'Is this the way to Delhi Square?' Ear to shoulder one side, ear to shoulder other side. Meaning half yes? Half no? I don't know? The young Indian doctor nodded like one of them, head up and down or back and forth. Yes. No.

He was New World. He had acquired his medical degree at McMaster University in Hamilton. He had also studied in

Boston and Chicago. If Mr. Gold had said they were Americans, the young Indian doctor would have told him about his Harvard sabbatical.

He had strong drugs. India had good drugs all the way around. 'Five days at most, she will feel much better, much much better.' He even touched Mr. Gold's shoulder, a tactic used by Western doctors. Mrs. Gold fretted in her room. She occasionally went to see Dana, but when she sat on Dana's bed all her daughter did was moan.

Rachel put the pills on Dana's tongue, held her head until she swallowed. Then she distracted Dana with stories of Rachel's favourite Romantic character, Lord George Gordon Byron. 'His lover Caroline Lamb sent him cuttings of her pubic hair in a love letter after Byron left her for Lady Oxford. Caroline Lamb desperately tried to call him back with her body, but she forgot to cast the charm of love. She should have put a spell on herself, which would have made the calling stronger. Instead, she lost her head in the begging. She wasn't thinking straight when she delivered to him a critical elixir ingredient. Her hair. Byron had his own tactile devices and also used hair as a romantic plot. His thick curls were worshipped. And his club foot brought on more quivering pity than any minuet. So it didn't matter that he couldn't dance. He solicited women's attention anyway—he stole them from their husbands or their lovers or their children. He was insatiable for women and boys and girls, most of all for his sister Augusta, who had his child. Don't think badly of him because of that, he didn't know her when they were little. He found her later. He died at sea. Such a romantic thing to do. Not now, though, Dana. It's not romantic for you. You're not that way. It would just be stupid. You see, one hour has passed and you haven't thrown up.'

THE TRAVEL AGENT CAME in a white nightgown and a black moustache. He came to sell Kathmandu to Rachel, parking his boat behind the bottleman's, who was selling a dark cola to Mrs. Gold. Nizme smiled. There would always be commission for him if something was sold.

The travel agent unfolded a map of Southeast Asia, an overview of the continent where India is pink, Nepal is blue. A cartoon bordering a kingdom. Even within the territories of these places boundaries are questionable: transient— negotiable—wars waiting—soldiers with guns all along the black broken lines. Forces to stop the unwanted from crossing, like the line Dana used to draw down the middle of the bed, the punishment a slap or a kick if Rachel trespassed. The more frequent the invasions or expeditions Rachel made across the line, giggling, the harder the slaps and kicks. Two world powers. A game—until real divisions were drawn through their lives, emotional sketches onto the fine lines of territories, until Rachel had night fears and had to sleep on the floor, on the line Dana had drawn outside her room. First a closed door and then a menacing voice. For a time there was a door alarm, then a string that snapped when anyone entered. Guards to Dana's room that went on being soldiers even when Dana wasn't home.

The travel agent unfurled a chart of Kathmandu. It wafted open like a cape. Not one a vampire would swing around his black wings, more like a glistening superhero cape, springing out at the back for effect. The map had been broken from a bigger geography. One that included the stars and the heavens. It was exaggerated in scale, something small blown up. It contained a city: circles for hotels, triangles for hostels, base camps red, the airport black. Stupas, Monkey Temple, Tibetan shelters for the monks who had run away from the Chinese government without an atlas, all their history in mandalas and bells. Buddha on fresh plaster.

Nepal was a slip in the mountains at the top of the Indian continent—at the top of the world. A blue hat on a pink body.

The key to this canvas is the air. It is thin. In some places where it is impossible to breathe, it is more conducive to dreaming.

The travel agent pointed to the centre of the town. 'I can make bookings for you.'

'I need pictures,' Rachel said. 'How do I know what I'm getting?'

'You know because you read in this book.'

'Yes, but I need to see a place.'

The travel agent laid out airmail stationery embossed with hotel insignias. 'You can see their paper.'

The *thangka* salesman had arrived and with the jewellery salesman already on the veranda with Mrs. Gold, sales were imminent. Adding to the clutter of maps around Rachel, the *thangka* salesman unrolled his sacred Buddhist paintings. After looking at dozens of canvases and bargaining, sitting in lotus position on the living room's fine Kashmiri rug, Rachel yawned. 'I can see you want the best quality,' said the *thangka* salesman. 'Here is the very oldest cloth, but also the most expensive. One hundred American dollars.' He uncurled a battered, blackened cloth; the paint was shrivelled and cracking. 'The *Sukhasiddhi Dakini thangka*, the Womb Door. To understand birth you must know all beyond.'

'Oh, I get it,' Rachel said of the bottle-eyed figure on the canvas displaying her red lippy vagina by hanging her feet up over her shoulders. 'Buddhist porn.' Her flippant remark defended against the painting's rumblings. It hypnotized her with its smoky green clouds. 'To know all beyond,' she said, 'you must know bliss. Bliss, nirvana, enlightenment, self-actualization are all unattainable. Buddha is elusive.'

Wanting to win Rachel's favour more than the few rupees the salesman would give as commission, Nizme crouched low beside her, very quietly and close to her ear: 'It's a fake. There are no old paintings left in Kashmir. It's been made to look that way. The antiquities were all stolen or sold. Now fresh paintings are smoked over charcoal fires to make the tourists happy.'

'But I can barely make out the picture,' Rachel said.

'Best-seller,' said the *thangka* salesman. 'We used to sell the fresh ones to travellers. Now we are a tourist city, they want antiquities. So we make them.'

'You can sell these souvenirs to the Americans,' Rachel said.

The travel agent, feeling forgotten, headed for his *shikara*. He left his maps under the pile of canvases. They could never be of use to Rachel, who had no sense of direction.

Rachel heard her mother speaking to a jewellery salesman

from the veranda. 'Oh, that's so cheap, maybe I should take more—for presents.'

After all the peddlers had left, Rachel stood looking out across Dahl Lake, trying to break her love thread to Lynton. At best, someday when she had lots of momentum, she would be able to throw the love off her. Some other young woman could catch it and go mad. Someone else could have rocks in her chest. It was winter somewhere. At the peaks of Kolahoi and Mahadiv it was cold, cold in the way that brought feelings to the surface—loneliness for instance. Zulkanyan slid the golden chain directly to Rachel to begin to administer sleep. The houseboat swayed in its mooring.

At night the lamplight blew across Dahl Lake in the direction of the market. Sewage from the city of Kashmir skimmed against the hull, mirror carp knocked there. The dust and debris of the day sank down through the water into shore silt. Invisible parasites like the ones that infected Dana floated on the water's surface. The things that couldn't be seen were taking over the world.

Suddenly Nizme was standing over Rachel, holding a wooden carving a German tourist had left behind: Ganesha, wearing a garland necklace, his elephant tusks paired with a man's body.

'They wrap the hash with newsprint soaked in jasmine oil, then stuff it up the hole and stop it with wood glue. Do you want to see?' He put his hand inside the deity.

Rachel shivered. 'Do you sell oil too?'

'Not me, them. They can get anything.'

'I know someone who came here and swallowed a kilo to bring it home. Didn't work, though. He might be dead for all I care what happened to him.'

When Lynton stopped making sense, he couldn't tell whether he was in India or Canada, or if his gut was full of drugs or he was just stoned. When he asked Rachel to forgive him over the phone, he didn't know if she was Rachel or Dana. Lynton had left Bombay clear-headed and landed at Dana's apartment in Vancouver, dry mouthed and dilated, as cherry cheeked as ever. Dana was studying for midterms. She had new friends. Lynton was an unwanted disturbance. He squatted, grunting over a kitty-litter tray, pushed out three latex condoms filled with hash oil, melted together by stomach acids. The rest of the kilo was slowly leaking pure uncut Kashmiri hash oil into Lynton's bloodstream. That was all Dana had to see to run him over to the airport. He slept until Toronto, mainlining from inside. The Canadian Pacific Air Line attendant couldn't wake him up, called an ambulance, sirens sounding more like his mother's grief when she found out than the prayer bells that were ringing in his head. The next morning a surgeon at Mt. Sinai Hospital opened Lynton's gut, took out the drugs and called the police.

Rachel felt inside the hollow wooden block. Red filing dust stuck to her fingers. She wiped it on her scarf.

'Tomorrow I can take you to the guru,' Nizme said. 'He's the one who made my father see.'

'But your father's blind.'

'Because he broke the secret and boasted to his friends.'

'Can't he go back and ask again?'

'He's used to it now. He says it's a blessing.' Nizme had a relentless stare that gave Rachel the shakes.

'I don't think I should go,' Rachel said. 'I don't keep secrets either sometimes.' That sounded stupid, she thought. She'd been saying silly things all day just to keep his eyes on her. She wanted help. Was keen to go to the guru and be saved but it didn't feel right. Nizme's father gave Rachel the creeps and her curiosity had not yet surpassed her fears. She was slowly coming to accept unexplainable events as part of the terrain. It seemed quite easy to imagine these things in India, where the Gods reminded Rachel of comic-book illustrations, assisted by garland wreaths and red dots.

In the hallway Nizme was clanging a spoon against a pot. A wake-up call to Rachel. Last night he crept into her room. He stayed for hours. It was his skin that fascinated her—his skin shadows. This would be just between the two of them. She wondered what gave these men the impression it was a right of passage for them all? Men without room for her independence, pinching her in the streets of Kashmir. Always the same lithe space between her legs, as long as they could not be seen, however they felt like it, one soft patch at a time, twisting up her flesh, then disappearing.

Rachel had been dug out by Lynton along with her flame. Dug out so deep it went to the other side. She needed to put someone, something, somewhere she could trust. Nizme?

She needed sex. In lovers' fluid, their DNA, she searched

the way seafaring treasure hunters did, putting down sonar lines for signs of matter in a vast ocean of blindness.

She needed to cry every morning as soon as she opened, so she could close a little. Enough so she could get out of bed and go.

She needed a cave, silver bracelets and rings. She needed fortune tellers to be in the world even if they were fakes.

She needed her mother not to be in her own little world.

Her love letters from Lynton were in her underwear drawer at home. She kept her underwear in a tallith bag, where men kept their prayer shawls. Her spoons were in with the tea bags, Nana's ruby in a snuff box. She kept her poems all over the place. Bills in the mailbox, for weeks.

There were certain things that everyone knew but her. Lots of things. Her blind patches. She needed someone who would help her to see and just as much, someone as blind as she was.

She could have done better if she had known, and if she had known she wouldn't have been the same; she would have been more common.

She hated logic but she liked the idea of it.

She needed to break rules because there wasn't any truth.

Maybe there was truth somewhere else in the world. Maybe she would find it further on in her travels.

She sensed eventually she would die of a broken heart— a broken thing, with that feeling of laughing and crying at the same time.

Rachel hadn't made love to Nizme. But she dreamt about it. It was a dream she made up while she was still awake. She wanted to tell him that the thought of him near her kept her up all night, she wanted to tell him she moved inside—in her heart and stomach, in her head. On the outside she was frozen.

Down the lake they floated on the morning prayers of the Kashmiri water boys. They paddled out past an array of houseboats and buoyant cucumber gardens, past homes hidden beyond a turn in the lake, Rachel shivering in the morning air, Nizme's single oar sinking deep into the water. He took off his sweater and handed it to her, then his bare arms joined again with the pace of the *shikara*. Rachel sniffed him in the sleeves of the sweater; she held her petite Minox camera in her lap.

A cluster of boats appeared in the foreground, some of them pointed like spears through the morning mist. It was just after sunrise. The boats hung around each other like a river outpost. Men were standing to barter for roots and onions, their hulls filled with vegetables cut from the shallow lake. Rachel and Nizme moved closer; three men sat together each on the prow of their open *shikara*. In the photo, one man prays. Rising smoke from a hookah pipe makes the face of another unreadable, and the third has his mouth full of potato.

On the way back to the houseboat, a child from a passing *shikara* reached out her hand. A lotus bloom spread over her tiny fist. A moment earlier she had picked the flower from the lake. Rachel liked the infant girl because she didn't speak; the child let the innocence of her face speak for itself. Her older brother, no more than ten, steadied their boat. The girl stretched her body. Rachel reached for the lotus intending to hand over a two-rupee note but the boats passed each other.

The child peered at Rachel. Eyes of a cicada.

Nizme turned the *shikara* around and grabbed the flower, gave it to Rachel.

She pulled it into her face.
A space in meditation.
Brilliant yellow, before an oncoming pale sleep.

When her face returned to its mean, beautiful self, as soon as she could keep water, when her legs woke up, Dana wanted to go home. Mr. and Mrs. Gold couldn't wait. They shouldn't have come to India, with daughters so sick of each other they couldn't behave long enough to get across a thin lake in a *shikara*. Rachel kissed her parents and said goodbye to Dana with a shrug. It was easier to love them now that they were leaving. It was also a relief for Rachel to unload her eight-hundred-page Lonely Planet guide to India. She stuck it on a shelf in the library next to the other two copies that had been abandoned.

RACHEL DIDN'T RECOGNIZE LENNART when she saw him at their meeting place in New Delhi. The Swede was thin, spoke slower than before. When he saw her, he smiled a great dark smile that made Rachel wonder if his teeth were rotting. A sad scary smile. 'Hello, Rachel. You look good.' A jack-o'-lantern grin. 'I bet it feels good to be free. By the way, I had a relapse of malaria while you were gone.' He smiled again; she saw the corner of a snuff bag under his lip. 'I almost died. It doesn't show, does it?' He spat. 'Sorry, sorry, I'm going to quit this habit when I get home.' He pushed the snuff back under his lip with his tongue. 'These sicknesses are unpredictable, you know. So much for chloroquine. I wasn't feeling myself, but who does out here. When I realized what was happening I was already in awful shape. I tried to go out and post a letter to my daughter. I vomited in the street, and then I was on the ground swimming in it. I guess the leper who was begging there didn't appreciate me, so he dragged me across the road. That corner was occupied by the local tooth extractor, who took me for his next customer. Stole all my rupees and pulled out a molar.' Lennart stroked his jaw. 'An Israeli from the hostel came by and carried me back spitting blood, which at first he thought was betel spittle. I love India. Can't wait to get out, though. What about you?'

Lennart was sure he was going to miss his plane. Then Rachel would take off to Nepal and he would be stranded. When he put his knapsack on the suitcase cart, he told her it would probably be lost on the way to Arlanda. At the last moment he took down Rachel's address. It was the beginning of the unknowing. What they had been through was now past and Lennart's assimilation back to Swedish life—from one type of dream to another—stepping out of red holy prayers into a navy blue night sky, travelling by Stockholm underground through rock, was the severing of the past. So maybe it was real and maybe it wasn't.

In the aeroplane lavatory, Rachel snatches little soaps out of a dispenser, splashes airline cologne around her neck, a cheap ocean to cover the sweat of a mountain crossing. She takes all the lipsticks out of her purse, opens them and lines them up, by shade, along the rim of the sink. She sits with her notebook in her lap, in the calm of the cubicle, sketching a photograph she took in Cairo. The scribble under The Arab in Front of the Tomb says:

*All you need to say is 'I know you.'*

IT WAS OFF-SEASON in the Kingdom of Nepal. The mountain climbers and hikers were regrouping in Tokyo, New York and Berlin. The tourists weren't there, only druggies and travellers who had no sense of time, those who took up local rituals as if they were their natural inheritance.

Freak Street was known.

When she stepped out of the Om Guest House on the first morning and looked up at the majestic Himalayas jetting up from Kathmandu valley, it was like the time she tried to figure out where the universe stopped. 'The inner desert,' Lhakpa Sherpa called it when he saw her awed expression. She told him how none of the tourists in Durbar Square were talking that morning, and she thought it was obviously the unspeakable beauty that shut them up.

She was tired. She had been uneasy since Israel, when training soldiers had crawled on their bellies in front of her beach towel in Natanya. Since then she kept coming across signs that said *Danger, Falling Rock* and *Avalanche Zone*. Lhakpa Sherpa said her soul was in shock and recommended that she see the yogi. 'And how many sticks of incense did you burn today?' he said waving his hands. The smoke in the room like the dust of dried fruit. Rachel moved across the cracked grey tiles of the deserted courtyard, then down the street and through a carved doorway framed with gold gilding and glittering red that said *Tibetan Massage*. Pictures of the yogi, his body stretched and posed, were pinned to the wooden walls. Rachel thought contortions like those were bound to bring on some kind of self-revelation or union with the divine. She trusted this yogi was well on his way to *samadhi*. When she was younger and Uncle Joseph was not so old, the two of them would practise a sequence of yoga postures attempting to relieve Uncle Joseph's strained back and bring spiritual purification to Rachel. 'If you say the *shmah* over and over again,' said Uncle, 'it will put you in a state of ecstasy, as will practising your breathing postures every day.'

The yogi's face was red-green, the colour of a ripening apple. His arms were brown, his muscle round. From across the room Rachel smelt the yogi's vegetarian body. She dropped her clothes and lay across his table. *My drugged soul.*

Not a word of English. Only *namaste*, and his hands. The yogi approached her slowly, looking for a sheet to peel back in stages over her body: her arms, breasts, a leg, the other one, down the stream of her stomach, her nape. Her sacrum hinging off his fingertips, her bum sitting in his hands, bent, a jackknife, his nostrils up in the air, down at her hip, between her it seemed. All he had was a small piece of cloth, which he tried to place across her breasts. It couldn't cover them so he moved the cloth down, resting it over her pubic V.

On his hands and knees like a leaping frog. Is he? A frog? Green-red. He cut a thin line into her dreams. Breathed them into him and back to her, into him and back to her, no longer a table or a concrete floor, the tip of a frozen mountain, his burning hands, losing her heat, cooling down so fast she went to sleep. Rocking, rocking.

It rained all night.

A flash of light.

The spirit Zulkanyan came landing on that sleeping night, *thunk*, in her head. Before Rachel had even reached Singapore. Zulkanyan slid himself into her head as an old man, when she was dreaming of the monkeys playing red drums at the Monkey Temple, the yogi squeezing her hand, after she burned incense on the window ledge. Rachel was visited by the spirit Zulkanyan after a flood of light in a setting sleep, with her eyes rolled back and her arm hanging over the bed. Cradled low in the valley, her life was down below the clouds. In the smoke. She was in the age of sleep that could happen at anytime, to anyone who is open like a snowing night.

The spirit Zulkanyan knocked at the door of her dream with a walking stick. *Knock, knock, knock.*

'Where is she?' he said.

'I don't know,' Rachel said. But she knew the woman he was looking for was dead and buried under the house. She didn't want the old man to find the body. Maybe it was her.

The part where Rachel opens the door to the house in her dream is the beginning of the rest of the story.

The spirit Zulkanyan went into her suitcase for maps. He poked his eye with one of his fingernails and filled it with blood. His finger became his pen. He flung blood across Java on her map of Indonesia, saying that for her safety Rachel was forbidden to go there. A place she had never been.

She screamed until she woke herself up.

Thinking it was her room that was possessed, Rachel

packed her bags and moved from a single-star to a four-star hotel. She immediately fell in love with the Tibetan monk who sold postcards in the lobby. Hanging over his nakedness was a scarlet robe.

The only time she left her bed now was to buy postcards. The monk smiled like he was loving her. He smiled like he loved everyone. And all the animals and plants, even the insects. Rachel never said anything to him. He was holy; she could feel it all up and down her spine. Even when she handed him the postcard for Lhakpa Sherpa she only said, 'Please go.' And then of course, '*Namaste.*'

She couldn't possibly send all the postcards she had bought, so she stuffed a pile of them under the tea tray in her room. A bunch of them she sent:

*Nana, the houseboats on Lake Dahl aren't really floating.*

*Lennart, I have been out night walking.*

*Lynton,*
 *I've always been the breath of others—more like them.*
This printed against the outline of Yeti's footprint in the snow.

THE IMPENETRABLE BLUE DRAPES were pulled over the Himalayas. The Nepalese doctor knelt by her bed. The post-card monk must have noticed her dwindling and told the hotel manager. 'I want to go home,' she said. 'I can't stand the light.' The doctor's breath was pastry dust. He approached her sleeping fever as if she were a broken thing. She told him about the pain over her heart, how it grabbed under her chest like a bear claw. How fits of sleep came without warning.

'There's no medicine for what's wrong with you,' he said. 'You can go home, but I don't recommend it.' Before he left he listened to her heart: *flub-flub, Dad tells me about God as he rocks me to sleep, all my legs hanging over his folded elbows. 'Believe in me.'*

She had been reading about the Gurkha's loyalty. How the British used them to fight their wars and then abandoned them without pensions. The fearless Gurkhas cut and sever.

When they draw their knives, the knife must taste blood, even if it is their own. The British blew things up, confused by shuffling tribal maps. The British didn't have the same lust for the whites of the eyes as the Gurkhas did; they went for the backs of heads.

Lhakpa Sherpa was banging on her door. 'Rachel, open up.' A hotel clerk had delivered a postcard from her.

*Feeling lonely.*
*Please come—Shangri-la Hotel.*
*Love*
*Rachel*
*P.S. Come now.*

She opened the door. A man staring at the face of a woman's weariness.

'Did you know the Gurkhas' *kukri* blade is curved for maximum ease to cut off heads?' were her first words.

'You read too much,' Lhakpa Sherpa said, observing the books around her bed. 'Guard the door,' said Rachel. She assumed he would know what hovered around the peaks of Everest. He would know the spirits who belonged there from the ones who didn't. Lhakpa Sherpa puffed out his hat, red and yellow. Stood it on his head.

The rain was barking at the door.

'Everything is connected, you know, Lhakpa. Not only that, but nothing's in order, even beauty isn't chronological. I will be beautiful when I'm old.' She began handing him things she didn't want to carry anymore: sandalwood shampoo, an Italian T-shirt, black soap, nail clippers, insect repellent and a pen.

Rachel wanted to walk out of the hotel but Lhakpa Sherpa saw her teetering and took her in his arms. He carried her out the door like a casualty, following the higher ropeways, in view of all the hotel guests. The monk was standing in front of the gift shop. He bowed to her; she tried to read his lips but couldn't.

Lhakpa Sherpa tucked Rachel into a taxi. He held her head as if he were keeping its contents from tumbling out. Her hair in black waves. In the quiet early morning, they moved along the road to the airport slower than a rickshaw. There were mountains in the clouds. Rachel was bloated with sleep in the arms of the Sherpa, who was smaller than her, smiling down. His muscles closed around her, digging into her sides. Rachel then found herself loving Lhakpa Sherpa the same way she loved the monk, loved Nizme, the same way she loved Nobody.

She was terribly afraid when Lhakpa Sherpa said goodbye at the airport and disappeared from sight. She held her purse close and walked to the centre of the terminal. She noticed that there was too much dust falling from the mountains; it never seemed to be cleared off the floors either. Everyone's shoes had dust on them. She was crumbling too, into the sur-rounding powder—alone—waiting in a room with forty or so Nepalese who were soon going to board planes. They sat together on benches by a window that gave a muted view of the Himalayas and a perfect panorama of the runway and air-port control tower. How much time before her plane left? Enough to go back to the room for a nap? Sitting on the benches were hundreds of shades of brown dust. Too many mothers peeling fruit.

She pulled on her Walkman headphones. Swaying back

and forth, hugging herself in, she said in her head, *There is a Western world*, and again, *There is a Western world. I come from there, it hasn't vanished.*

Since Lhakpa Sherpa left, nothing moved out there. *Quiet birds.* There were air restrictions. After the advent of aeroplanes, air became a tangible element. Planes were tracked on radar screens. Height limits and sound disputes, residential resistance to jets screaming overhead as people worked in their gardens. As a child it seemed to Rachel that the airways were invaded by the thoughts and feelings of strangers and strange places.

Air space can be rented from governments or sold in tanks for water-breathing. Hard to obtain mountain visas where oxygen is scarce. Hidden resources come into dispute when they are valuable. *There is a Western world. I came from there, it hasn't disappeared.*

# Book II

THE ONE WORD SHE LANDED on the island with she had picked up from a couple in Greece, and then again from an Arab in New Delhi. It had meant nothing to her, yet she had tucked the name into her mind because of the way it was said—imbued with ethereal promise, dire passion, lost cause. Her suitcase lined with *thangka* scrolls rode down the carousel. She rolled the name around in her head like a mantra. From the back seat of a taxi, more loudly than the sound of the day's rain threading through the tires on the black paved road, she said 'Raffles' to the driver as if she knew all about it—when it was still only a word. What she did know was that the eyes of travellers jumped when they said it, stoned or enchanted, they grabbed Rachel's arm, pulling her into them, insisting, 'You absolutely have to.'

Rachel still had clouds in her head, trooper's blood, adventure lust wandering her veins. Glee in her heart, she counted her luck, repeating loudly to herself, 'Raffles,' the way the others had said it to her, the word now a place. At the front steps, she stood looking up. It was a Himalayan mountain rising from the flat surface of the island. Tall, tall, turns of timber. Three thousand two hundred and fifty-six window mouldings. An old fort. A chef's palace. A hang-out-hideout, with an orange aura. Above the hotel the Southern Cross was embedded in the sky, multitudes of shadows lurking.

Nothing seemed more fictitious than old Raffles Hotel, but it was real, and to its very bone in front of her. Textures of white surfaces teemed off the dark corridors, gleaming. It was one of those rare exalted architectures that swallowed human frailty with compassion (being a dishevelled master-piece itself), instead of turning away vulnerability at the front door. This is more than a hotel, Rachel thought, it's a love affair.

For a moment she was overcome with premonitions. They tumbled and tingled inside her. She stroked the small leather medicine pouch that she had pulled out from under her shirt. Halfway across the world and halfway home, certainly that meant something.

The skeletal night staff slid to the reception desk of the sleeping hotel. Rachel knew not one person in Singapore, had never read about the place, save for her science project on rubber plantations in seventh grade. 'How much is a room?' she said to the clerk.

'One hundred and sixty Singapore dollars.'

'How much is that?'

'About one hundred and thirty American dollars.'

'I don't know how long I'm staying.'

'May I see your passport?' When she turned to rummage through her sack, Rachel noticed a man behind her fidgeting with his keys. She barely acknowledged him until the clerk said, 'He says he's with you.'

'No, I don't know him.'

'No?'

'I saw him at the airport. He showed me where the taxi stand was.'

The agitated clerk began screaming at the man, in Mandarin, which made it sound worse than it really was. It sounded catastrophic. On top of everything Rachel noticed the clerk was missing two fingers on his left hand.

Then Kifli Talib stepped out from behind a wall.

He picked up Rachel's suitcases and they slipped away, up the back stairs to her room.

She didn't pay any attention to the Malay porter, that he left without a tip or that she had arrived at the open door in her dream. The door latch was loose, the phone in her room old, black and heavy. She picked it up and put the receiver to her ear. 'Raffles front desk.' 'Oh sorry, I'm just testing the line.' She removed a piece of thin hotel stationery from the writing-desk drawer and spied her hand through it. Tinkling ice in a Campari on the desktop, under a swirling fan, she wrote, *I am Somerset Maugham*. It was better to live literature than to read it, better to sleep in a mausoleum whose mattresses hadn't been changed for decades.

Rachel writes to Lynton. She puts *Dear* on the page, then *Lynton* after that. *Dear Lynton*. That is all. She sits in front of the page for at least twenty minutes without writing a thing. In her mind she says,

*My love,*
*You have never been to Singapore—so it is all mine.*
She presses the glass to her lips. She loves the look of a thick ruby splash in a crystal highball.

*Dear Lennart,*
   *I imagine you have just returned to Sweden, to (girl-friend) and your little girl. How was the flight? I have just arrived at Raffles in the dead of night. This room is half the size of a field hockey pitch.*
   *Had a terrible fright at the airport in Nepal, the dust came tumbling off the mountains like an avalanche.*
   *Take care, my friend.*
   *Love*
   *Rachel*
   *P.S. Write to me at the American Express office in Sydney.*

By the time she went to bed her things were strewn all around her hotel room: red nail polish, violet cotton sari, sandals and shoes, *Magister Ludi* by Hesse, and Rabindranath Tagore's *Gora*, published by S. G. Wasani for Macmillan India Limited, open to page 7, where Rachel had marked a passage for a postcard to Nana.

   *'I see clearly enough that you are treading the path of weakness.'*
   *'Weakness indeed!' Binoy exclaimed irritably. 'You know well enough that I could go to their house this very moment if*

*I wanted to—they have even invited me—and yet you see I do not go.'*

*'Yes, I know. But you never seem able to forget that you are keeping away. Day and night you are harping on it to yourself: "I do not go. I do not go!" Better far to go and be done with it!'*

THERE SHE LIES. BREATHING in increments barely measurable—comfortable to observe. Her eyes are open but she is asleep. She alternates between that state and a mild wakefulness where she understands the morning has passed. She has been having episodes during the day in which she fades out, when stillness insists itself and time is whimsical. It's always raining, and rain contains sleep. When she inhales deeply the air cuts through her heart. When her breathing is shallow and slow, the pain over her heart subsides. She has no name for her condition.

Her first morning in Singapore she is buried under a stone that pins her to the bed. To wake up Rachel has to fight her way through rock. She feels no obligation to move. She has no will to be awake in a room where she is alone. When the housekeeper arrives at noon to make the bed, she calls through the door.

Traversing veins of rock while climbing to the surface, Rachel sees a man wearing a viper's hood walking in the rain.

THERE HE LIES. BREATHING in increments barely measurable—comfortable to observe. His eyes are closed but he is awake. The spirit Zulkanyan was right when he told Kifli that the woman of the enemy would arrive in the middle of the night. Finally, she is here. Kifli won't have to work the night shift for a while. Now he will have time to study for his hotel management exam. He will work the morning shift on Mondays and Thursdays. A textbook is open next to Kifli on the bed. If he wants to sell the book after he is finished with it he better not use a highlighter or a pencil to underline important points, so he writes them into a workbook. *Your staff must be pleasant and courteous, wear a clean, well-pressed uniform and have neat hair and clean fingernails. Always try to help your staff so they will be willing to come to you with any problems. If you don't know what to do, call in a senior manager who will assist.* To summarize this paragraph Kifli has written in his workbook, *Be a Singaporean.*

Outside his window the government-landscaped gardens of his parents' apartment block are rooted in a thin layer of ground cover imported from Malaysia.

He had seen Rachel's dark hair and her silver bangles in a

vision before he met her. Not her face. He couldn't make it out through the shadowy haze. No vision ever brought to him her spicy perfume oil. What did he know about this kind of woman? White, Western, travelling alone as ·if she has the right to all her own movements and decisions. And she does, it seems, have that right. No one is stopping her. Her father and mother allowed her to go off into the world. There is no one from her family looking over his shoulder.

He senses that Rachel has powerful magic. Kifli feels strange. Dizzy and weak in his stomach. He imagines Rachel again and again, smiling and joking about the weight of her luggage, which she told him drives everyone crazy. He imagines her smile settling over him, warm and vulnerable. She is the scariest thing Kifli has ever seen. He never thought the enemy would try to overthrow him without violence and hatred and blood. This is the unexpected subtlety of the Jew, that Rachel's smile moved in on him like cooking smoke penetrating its meat, inseparable, then, from flesh.

Even with his eyes closed, today he is hyper-aware of his pockmarked face. If she'd missed it in the dark, next time she would notice right away.

After working the night shift Kifli usually has the day off, but he has told himself that he has to put in extra hours to make up for the time he will miss studying for his exam. He can't sleep anyway.

RACHEL HAD BEEN WANDERING around the city without delving into it, avoiding the cubby-hole streets where the shops' merchandise was crammed on shelves or hanging tightly together, saris and tablecloths, Versace silk prints that had disappeared from the factory in India and reappeared in Singapore, reams of cloth on bolts, set up like webs for customers to admire and suffocate in. Instead of bargaining for value in the Indian bazaar or the Chinese market, Rachel walked along Orchard Road where she could be surrounded by a sense of commerce with order. The order Singapore was famous for, set up for tourists and wealthy Singaporeans who were willing to spend for sterile space, designer clothing, leathers and politeness.

At Charles Jordan of Paris Rachel bought a pair of green suede shoes. She told the saleswoman to keep the shoes in the box. Digging her nails into the flesh of a chicken at lunch she watched the shoebox on the chair next to her. Later she would pace her suite as if she were modelling the green elfin shoes for a guest.

What beautiful shoes. Dancing shoes, street shoes, decadent Parisian wear-the-expensive-shoes-in-the-jungle shoes.

When the box flew open, the saleswoman's trapped perfume rose from the deep moss of the shoes. She slid her feet into the leather.

WITH HER DARKNESS RACHEL bent over the stranger. She thought the odds were good that the young woman sitting at the café was American or perhaps Dutch. She looked down into the plain face wearing a wide-brimmed hat in the drizzle as if the sun were haunting her delicate skin. Rachel had owned a hat like that once, when she was six or seven—a sign of soft language that didn't curse, an announcement of vulnerability.

'I love your hat,' Rachel said.

'Thank you. It's my mother's gardening chapeau.'

'How nice of her to lend it to you.'

'I didn't have one of my own.'

Rachel shrugged, how extremely tired she was. Her hand pointed to the empty chair opposite the American, who quickly nodded. 'I'm Catherine. I'm from Minnesota, a Christian singing with my church choir.' Rachel teetered on the edge of her seat. 'Really,' she said. Catherine took Rachel's hand, lovingly, as a traveller from home who was homesick might do, or a Christian looking for souls, spreading Rachel's bracelets up along her tanned arm.

Earlier that afternoon Rachel had seen the white faces of street entertainers standing out against the Asian sky. She imagined Catherine dancing in a whirlwind for God, her long blond hair floating around her face like the bronze mask of a river Goddess. Catherine was beige, almost translucent. A curiosity under a hat. In Toronto Rachel wouldn't even have noticed her; Rachel's eyes would have been drawn to heavier beauty, a slick bicycle courier or a bare-armed female boxer running pavement, a billboard of Christ with his arms spread out over Bay Street asking for more men for the seminary.

'I can't talk about God today,' Rachel said, 'but I haven't spoken to an American in months. It's all broken English out here. The same simple words over and over. You could lose your own language and then you'd be stuck. I could have slept all day, but they had to clean the room. I'm staying at Raffles—and you? Have you been away long?'

'Two months.'

'It's not the length of time anyway, is it? I've only been away five or six months, and I can't remember what it's like to drive a car.' She bent her head back over the cusp of the chair.

Catherine adjusted the exaggerated bow on her hat. 'When I go home I'm going to get my parents back together.'

'Oh.' Rachel twisted her hair into a bun behind her neck. Let it fall. 'I'm really sorry.'

'That's okay. I think they just figured out everything there is to know about each other. Sometimes love dries into dust. For years the only thing I remember between my parents is my father moaning when he ate my mother's chocolate cake.'

'With chocolate icing?'

'That's the only time he looked at her that way. You know, like he loved her.'

'Maybe he blames her for everything,' Rachel said. 'I think that's what happened to me and Lynton.'

'Your husband?'

'No way, not since he became my sister's lover.'

'Oh my.' Catherine put her hand to her mouth.

'Yeah, as bad as that. So your father ran off with his secretary?'

'He's a farmer.'

'Really? Huh. Funny, I didn't know farmers got divorced. They're so committed, coming back to the same fields year after year.'

'I think it's the winter.'

'Actually, I shouldn't compare a woman to a crop,' said Rachel. 'We're really more connected to the sea than the earth, don't you think? You know, the way we're always drowning.'

'Why can't we just be like ourselves?'

'Absolutely,' Rachel said. 'I agree. It was just a metaphor. I guess that means fishermen get divorced too.'

'Oh no, they're forever married to the sea. They don't even have wives.'

Rachel moved forward in her chair and took Catherine in again. 'Hey, that was a good one,' she said.

'Thanks.'

'I've never seen my father naked,' said Rachel.

'Neither have I,' said Catherine. A pause. The idea of it.

'Well, I saw him in his underwear lots of times,' Rachel said. 'But that doesn't count. I grew up on a farm too. Life there's so heartbreaking, animals passing through this world faster than us. One summer my sister, Dana, found Orville the mouse in a bale of hay. He was only a few days old. A little pink thing. His eyes weren't even open yet. He was motherless. We wrapped him in Kleenex and put him in a matchbox. Then he wouldn't eat from the eyedropper. He was so small it was hard to find his mouth. When Orville died a few days later we buried him behind the woodpile in the matchbox he had passed away in. We declared him an angel and marked his grave with a lucky stone.'

'Animals are God's children too,' Catherine said.

Her parents' divorce was all over her. It made Rachel feel that sinking kind of emptiness she felt on Sunday mornings. That something vital to her happiness was missing and she was never going to find it.

'You're a mercenary?' Rachel said.

'No, a missionary.'

'What's the difference?'

'Mercenaries are paid soldiers.'

'I *see*, and missionaries don't...' She stopped herself from continuing to say that everyone should have the restraint to keep their religion to themselves, if they had to have one at all. She was borrowing Catherine's kindness for a moment of sanity. She didn't want her cynicism to steal these few seconds of home from a whitewashed American. Catherine was harmless. A lamb. If only she could help Rachel out of her sleeping sickness. Rachel looked at the sky. 'Does the rain affect your singing?'

Catherine smiled. She perched one hand on top of Rachel's. Rachel's pulse ran fast and wiry. 'Here's a song a Jewish gypsy wrote,' Catherine said, and then she dropped the prayer for rain and the prayer for dreams. They fell onto the floor, crawled under the table and disappeared beneath the soles of Rachel's elfin suede shoes, where streaks of a fleshier green had been rubbed back. The words came to Rachel through her feet.

*There are two ways the rain may fall. Af, in brutal torrents, a sign of divine anger, and Bri, in prosperity, nurturing the soil. Af-Bri is the angel of the rain clouds.*

The question lingered in Rachel's head, *Am I awake or am I sleeping?*

Flecks of pastry dough crumbled from Catherine's lips.

In the silence that followed Rachel must have dozed off. She knew that when she slept, her soul fed her blood. From the beginning it was the things she couldn't control that possessed her: Lynton, Pink Bunny's last breath, the flying squirrel in the boys' cabin at camp, the fear of the times-table flash cards at school, the smell of roses from her nanny's kisses, the voices calling her name on the way home from school, and the dragon-winged cicada crawling out of its skin, standing helpless on its old shell, waiting for new silver wings to harden.

The insect dragged its curly arms. Smelling like a cable car. Rachel discovered it, halfway in, halfway out of its old skin. It looked up at Rachel and said, 'I have so little time to get out of here before I will be encased in my own skin like a tomb.' The cicada arched its back to further split its exoskeleton, raising its yellow meaty breast which contained a substantial heart.

The insect stood on its old crusty form. 'I've grown shiny wings.'

'If you don't get out of the sun,' Rachel said, 'you're going to bake on the sidewalk.'

'I can't move just now no matter what happens. My wings need to set.'

Rachel leaned over the insect to shade it. She became an umbrella. The cicada told Rachel its moulted skin was good for lost voices. 'Keep it, it makes a sweet tea.'

Each succeeding summer Rachel would happen across a pungent shell and jump in her step. Another dragon cicada had escaped on metallic wings to sound the sun alarm.

Rachel incorporated the protruding eyes of the dragon insect into her shadow, along with the essence of childhood impressions that resembled charcoal drawings. At times Rachel was paralyzed by contradictions in the collective memories and discoveries that filtered through her.

Lynton knew about her passionate fears. He had them too. 'It's just your age,' the doctor had told him after his suicide attempt. Soon after Lynton was released from the hospital he went to a deserted cabin on a rock island at Pointe au Baril. A cottage that had been vacant for a generation. Lynton related to the place. He left the dust where it was, it had been piling up fine for ten years. He avoided disturbing the spiders. No phone, a boat ride to the post office, no one to care how much hash he smoked or to stare at his scar when he took off his shirt in the sun. Even though he was living the life he wanted, sometimes he felt closed in. That's when he visited the main house and snooped. He read old magazines advertising health tonics and Dodds liver pills, and he studied maps of the area left on top of the stone fireplace.

He preferred the size of the guest cabin in the woods. A wood-burning oven heated the two rooms, the front porch and the bedroom where Lynton kept his writings in a black pouch under the bed. He winterized the cabin by nailing handmade patch quilts to the walls. He stored his cooking oats there, between the wood and the cotton.

Rachel went to say goodbye before she left on her travels. When he saw her he said, 'What are you doing here—no, really, what? I can't do it.'

'Don't be silly,' she said. 'I'm already dead. I'm a walking ghost.' Lynton turned around in the moccasins Rachel had smuggled into the psychiatric ward—scarlet deerskin, the colour of their bonding, Rachel thought, much darker than Lynton's cherry cheeks. 'Lynton,' she said, 'what can I do to you?'

For three days she wore only Lynton's blue Viyella shirt. 'Why do you have to get out of bed?' she said. 'It's early.'

'I have to fix the roof.'

'Now?'

'Would you rather I wait till it rains?'

'I'll help you then.'

'You don't have to. You're afraid of heights.'

'I don't have any fears since my worst fears came true.'

Lynton didn't answer. She followed him up the ladder and watched until she thought she had the hang of it. She picked up some roof tiles, nails and a hammer, hammered her thumb. Lynton stood there laughing at her with her finger in her mouth. She hadn't heard him laugh in a long time, seen how his eyes light up their beautiful blue. Rachel laughed too. They stood on the roof together in hysterics while Rachel's thumb ballooned with blood. What they would normally have done after a scene like that no longer made sense, words they would have said were now forbidden; still, she wanted him so badly. He, too, her. In their silliness, they forgot the hurt between them, and in the same joke, suddenly, they remembered it again. He tore off his clothes and went to her. She could never refuse him. He lifted the Viyella shirt over her head. 'Oh my God, Rachel.'

She crouched in pain.

'We have to do something.'

'What does that mean?'

'Well...'

'What are you saying?'

'I can do it.'

'How?'

'The hand drill.'

'Through my finger? Are you crazy?'

'Jesus, Rachel, we have to take the pressure off.' He grabbed the drill.

'What are you doing?'

'I'm changing the bit.'

'What if you don't pull back on time?'

'I will.'

'You don't know what you're doing.'

'I've done it before.'

'When?'

'To myself.'

'Let's go to the hospital.'

'We don't have time.'

'Sure we do.'

'Rachel, for fuck's sake, look at your hand. Give it to me.'

'I don't trust you,'

'I know, give me your hand.'

'Fuck off.' She gave it to him.

'Look over my shoulder.'

'I wish you were dead.'

'So do I.'

'Liar.'

'Look over my shoulder, Rachel, not at me.'

'Okay,'

'I'm sorry.'

'What?'

'I'm sorry.' And then he burned a drill bit through her nail. The blood shot up into the air like in the movies. Bright blue-red blood.

'I think I'm going to throw up.'

'Okay, that's okay.' She fainted instead. Lynton lay on top of her so she wouldn't fall off the roof. She started to return almost immediately.

'God, I'm sorry, Rachel.'

'I did it to myself.'

'Come on, let's get some ice.'

'Lynton.'

'What?'

'What did I say just then?'

'Nothing, you were mumbling.'

'I know, but what did I say?'

'You said, "Save me," Rachel. I can't save you.'

The morning Rachel motored away from Lynton, she couldn't hear a thing. The leaves were silent in their fall. Without him her world was gone. She had the sense that small things were big—even enormous. The previous evening Rachel swallowed a lock of Lynton's hair, incorporating Lynton's essence, his genetic map, into her body to ward off the unbearable feeling of separation. *There is no vocabulary for what we keep in our blood from experience.*

Catherine was on her toes singing about Jesus. *Jesus, Jesus.*

A white-faced mirage. A kiss on Rachel's cheek. 'He's in my blood now,' Rachel said. 'I guess I'm in crisis.'

'Crisis is how we come to Christ,' Catherine said. For the first time her faith made sense to Rachel.

'Crisis is the moment you realize you've been betrayed.'

'I don't hate anyone,' Catherine said.

'No, I can't imagine that you do, yet.'

Two young women, a Christian and a Jew, blond and black, with a blue-eyed Christ who was dead and a Messiah who was yet to come. Both saviours seductive like fathers.

It might have occurred to them that day that their search was their commonality, both plodding through some kind of man hocus-pocus trying to get to their own splendour. Unlike Catherine, Rachel wanted to see what her powers—good, bad, subtle or whip-sharp—were all about. She sensed Catherine's innocence would stay with her for a long time, but Rachel was trying to shake hers off so she could—see clearly.

The sky was ready to break its fever and rain again. Rachel scurried up the steps to Raffles Hotel, the flap of her sack flung open by the monsoon wind. The Malay porter held out her room key. It hung from a short chain and slid into her hand, clenched instantly out of sight. She hardly saw his image, just the bluntness of his black hair.

The rain sizzled at the windows of the hotel's Long Bar where the bartender had made Rachel a gin sling. When she thought of Lynton, she sat so still it was as if she were simply an ornament at the table.

*Dear Lynton,*
    *I have been to India too. And I have recovered from idolizing you and your pain. Still, I can't stay awake and I dream about you. I wake up smelling you. I imagine your small hands under my dress.*
*Rachel*

IN A DESERTED STRETCH OF HALLWAY she knelt down to sniff the teak floorboards, inhaling lemon oil wood polish, trying to loosen the Indian monsoon from her sinuses.

In her room she shed her clothes. The dampness of the air weighed the creases out of the same T-shirt she had worn in the desert at Nebulas. She lifted the white sheets half off the bed and slid in, plummeting to sleep at four o'clock in the afternoon. Half an hour later the phone rang. 'Kifli Talib from hotel reception.' The Malay porter made his formal introduction across a wire.

'Who?' she said.

'A man has come to see you.'

'I don't know anyone.'

'He came with you last night.'

'I don't know him.' She couldn't get the words out, *I'm still sleeping*.

'I want to move you closer to reception. I'll send someone.'

'When?'

'Now if you like.'

The front desk seemed a long way off—unattainable if things went wrong. Beyond her back door tree ferns waved in a cool speeding madness—wild shadows of the day overgrown from the rain. Rachel remembered her afternoon dream. *Soldiers crawling on their bellies up the hill of her parents' front lawn. The curtains, closed across the glass house. Rachel's semi-automatic is propped up on white down couch pillows. There is a frogman waiting at the back door to take her into the water.*

Kifli is crouched, passing a note under the rosewood door of her new suite. She pulls up the paper so fast that his hand is still touching it on the other side.

> *A hotel guest has offered me a job in Vancouver.*
> *Could I meet you to talk about Canada?*
> *Kifli Talib (hotel reception)*

Now it is personal between them.

He rings her a second time. Must have raced back to the front desk and dialed her room number. Not enough time to study his handwriting.

'It's me, Kifli.' His voice is hollowed out over the phone, as if it is coming from the centre of a pacific volcano.

'Have we met?'

'I gave you your key at the front desk.'

'Oh.'

'How do you like Singapore?'

'I don't really know.'

'Well, anyway, someone offered me a job and if you don't have plans for dinner, I thought...'

'No.'

'Oh, okay then. Maybe another...'

'No, I mean I don't have plans. What time is it?'

'Half past six.'

'What about eight?'

'I'll come for you then.'

IN ROOM 107 AT THE PALM COURT, Rachel tossed herself into the evening, waking periodically and reading from a tourist book.

> *Thomas Raffles was born at sea.*
>     *The Armenian Sarkies brothers built Raffles Hotel.*
>     *Joseph Conrad, who was then a seaman, was one of their first patrons.*
>     *Dozens of electric fans were installed in the stately Grand Ballroom making it 'the coolest ballroom in the East.'*
>     *As Singapore surrendered to Japan, British colonialists gathered at Raffles singing 'There'll Always Be an England.'*
>     *The kitchen staff scrambled to find hiding places for silver goblets and trays in the gardens.*
>     *Strewn across straw mats on the back lawn, malnourished beriberi victims were sprayed with disinfectant by Japanese medics.*

Raffles Hotel began as a dream under a fez. Peeling plaster walls and creaking rattan lounges still alluded to ballroom femmes fatales sulking about in sleeveless chiffons prior to the Japanese occupation.

Rachel had walked in at the perfect time. Raffles was no longer pristine and no longer mobbed by dignitaries and hoity-toity tourists. Couches still wore their original fabric. All over the city towers were being constructed with grand lobbies, carpet to chandelier, and facades that one-upped each other. Singapore in the mid-1980s had more hotel rooms than inhabitants. Raffles had been forgotten, had become a peeling edifice. Like Rachel, it was unsure of its place in time.

The days of palm fans tied to wagging servant toes to clear the heat from sweaty British brows were over. And Rachel couldn't help but imagine that she was a fair-minded woman alone in the virgin regions of Asia waiting for temptation, where cynical writers had chosen to reside and curse colonialism, projecting themselves instead into the more romantic Orientalism while swigging back slings. Rachel was sure there must be one tiger left on the island, to be shot, oh so handsomely, as in the past, under a pool table at Raffles.

'Oh,' she wanted to say, 'there's a tiger about. It must be trapped and taken back to the jungle.' The doormen and porters uniformed in Gieves & Hawkes would be frantically running around the grounds with at least one gentleman diligently guarding Rachel's door. There must be a search in every secret corner, under china cabinets and behind hidden doors. The Bras Basah wing must be scoured including all the back service verandas. Perhaps even the sacred private rooms of Charlie Chaplin and Jean Harlow, for their protection, of course. A wild tiger is breathlessly beautiful but deadly just the same.

And on that day more would be discovered about the goings-on in Singapore than in the whole of its tiny British history. During the scuttle, Rachel imagined she would wrench some young boy's heart with her charms.

KIFLI TALIB STOOD AT HER DOOR holding a pink orchid as if it were potted in his hand. He had the hands of a ballerina. Slender, long and malleable.

'For you, Rachel Gold.' He was taller than she expected from his voice on the phone.

'Now I remember you,' she said, pushing the door wide open to take a closer look at him. Kifli was framed by the view of the Palm Court at dusk; patio lights moved across his face as if fish tails splashed across it. Skin laden with pockmarks. His lips an elliptical sable heart. His eyes the same darkness as her own, an easy sight to endure.

'So you're the man who's protecting me.' She offered her hand, he placed the flower in it casually. Rachel crushed the pink petals between her fingers.

'It won't die,' he said. 'It's silk.'

'No, well, thanks. Come in.'

As soon as the Malay porter stepped across the threshold of her room, Rachel saw he was a man-boy. She began to fidget. She excavated her purse for money and passport. 'I'm reading Hermann Hesse. Look,' she said, and vanished into the bedroom. She turned back the sheets of her bed and retrieved *The Glass Bead Game*, a paperback stained with tanning oil, pages flimsily hanging off a cracked spine. 'His name is on the door—Hesse has slept in this room. Fate has brought us together. I'm feeling better already.'

'You look tired.'

'It's nothing, just the heat. Such a modern city you have here, I had no idea. I guess I wasn't ready for it.'

'But you're from Canada?'

'I keep thinking about my car, wondering if I'll remember how to drive when I get home. The idea of a highway seems so odd, so crazy. Where are all those people going?'

'What are you doing in Singapore, Miss Rachel Gold?' It seemed to Kifli she was completely alone. And how was it he felt like he knew her?

'I don't know. I seem to be following my feelings around. It's what we do when we finish university.'

He smiled blankly back at her. 'Have you seen the ballroom yet?'

'Do you think I can find myself there?' He giggled nervously. 'I'm only kidding,' she said, dipping her hand back into her purse. 'Where did I put my key?'

'It's on the writing table,'

'How do you know?'

'I can see it. Are you all right?'

'Yes, of course, I'm just a little tired.' She scooped up the key. 'Thanks for the room. It's...wow...it's...' She scanned the room. 'It was very kind of you.'

'You'll be safer with people around.'

'Is it dangerous?'

'In Singapore? No, you are very safe as a woman alone.'

SPINNING ON THE ENDS OF POLES, ceiling fans akin to single-engine propellers slit the air and twisted it over the Grand Ballroom. Little bulbs from chandeliers cast yellows on the tables. Here, from the beginning, solid trysts and decadent costume balls were accompanied by jazz or big band, or Charlestons performed by flappers in red fringe or white beaded chiffons. Elite Chinese patrons dressed as British gentlemen and the whites decked out as coolies. Rachel got it right away, every little sin that went down. Regrettably, she wasn't there. She is there now, when the Ballroom is empty. Except for her and Kifli Talib.

He handed her an old menu. She tongued the words with her eyes.

*Kedah fowls*
*Bengal mutton*
*Java potatoes*
*Salted turtle eggs*

The words filled her up, as fragrant words are edible. 'Do you cook, Kifli?'

'Sometimes I help my mother make noodles.'

'She must love you for that.' Rachel extended her hand. 'Do you dance?'

'Not rock and roll. I dance in a customary way.'

In the middle of the empty dance floor, he turned his face sharply toward Rachel and spun his eyes to the back of his head. He dropped into a squat, then careened across the Carrara marble floor in a series of precise Silat movements. The fighting art of *Perisai Diri*. His hands delivering punishment to an invisible foe. With electric force he administered the thrust-punch, claw-hand and knife's edge. He exhaled vigorously, ending with an eye tear and neck twist, hurling the limp enemy to the ground. Still frozen in his final pose he looked away from his fallen adversary, to her.

Much more than she had thought, no longer a shy boy, rather a flamboyant, articulate performer filled with hidden knowledge. Rachel had underestimated him. He wasn't the tuxedo clean cut she would normally have cast herself onto the dance floor with, better yet, he was deceptively understated. She was all out in the open. Rachel sensed she wasn't in control of this fantasy. If she was, she wouldn't be shaking, or trying to hide her lust.

She felt him calling her water—so she spoke about the desert in Nebulas. 'Even a few yards can seem miles away... Pumping stations are fenced in and guarded by soldiers... Water feeds everything doesn't it, Kifli? Even the soul.' Just as Rachel finished speaking Catherine's prayer crept up through her feet, her legs, and flowed, an incomprehensible smoke, without her even knowing it, out through her belly button. It surrounded her, the infinite shape of a golden mean spiral.

*Af-Bri is the name of the angel of rain designated to form and thicken clouds, to empty them and to cause water to fall.*

Kifli was nervously looking at his hands. Rachel's water filled her mouth. She swallowed hard. Her eyes were wet. She didn't want to look back at him anymore. He took in some air. Exhaled into another smile. There was nothing about him she could read.

*May Af-Bri bring us portions of segregated rain, to soften the wasteland's face when it is dry as rock. To soothe with its drops those to whom was blown a soul.*

And then like the clap of a hoof on a monsoon stone the cumin-skinned Kifli Talib faced the travelling scarab lover Rachel Gold and said, 'I am a Muslim. And you, Rachel Gold, I think are a Jew?'

'Yes, yes, I am. What about it?'

'Nothing. I just wanted to know.'

He comes forward as if to whisper to her, turns his face in slowtime. She feels the heat from his lips, tastes his breath, a kiss. Sable to her lips. After his lips withdraw he retreats too.

*Angels are composed of fire and water. When you pass through water I am with you. When flames engulf you, you shall not be burned.*

Rachel turned to the slightly cooling night. The kiss had already disappeared as if it had never happened. Something odd. An empty kiss without sex behind it. A kiss without lingering.

'There are people here who would kill me if they knew who you were,' he says. 'I want you to know I don't hate Jews.'

'I know, I know, it's the same everywhere.'

'I've been taught to hate you, but I won't.'

'What is there to hate?' she said. 'You don't even know me.'

And true to her afternoon fantasy, that evening Rachel knew complete unremorseful desire when Kifli Talib escorted her, like an old-fashioned gentleman, around the corner to the A&W, where they ate fried chicken fingers with hot chili sauce.

He had also taken her to the market and given her rose water and violet water to drink. He held a star fruit out to her on his flat palm as if it were a living creature illuminated from inside. Its skin was as soft as a spaniel's belly. Rachel didn't know if it was plucked from a branch like a banana—easier to imagine the fruit for its name, lending light to the night sky.

At the door of her room Rachel reached out and touched Kifli lightly on the nose. 'You are beautiful,' he said. There was no motive behind his observation. He simply stated what he saw, having never been so close to a white Western woman, not long enough to look so carefully and leisurely, before he walked away. Because he couldn't pursue her.

From behind the front desk he had watched her tangible face in the light; right away his heart crushed against his long bone ribs. He noted the urgency with which she fled. Her exhaustion. What he took from her eyes was her willingness to undo herself to find meaning.

He wanted all of her and he never wanted to see her again, there was nothing in her eyes for him anyway. She would probably tell him about her boyfriend, like he wasn't even there. And he was already making a list of his faults: his old shoes, the pockmarks on his face that would always be the first thing anyone saw. She made him uneasy. He did stupid things like blowing wind into his stories. He wasn't a businessman, didn't go so far in school. He could never fascinate her as much as the spirit Zulkanyan would when he appeared, and he would show himself soon. Kifli just knew that.

After she shut the door, Rachel shook herself off like a wet dog. She was imagining all of it. A Muslim kissing a Jew.

KIFLI STRIDES AWAY ACROSS the back lawn of Raffles Hotel, through the black trees behind the sleeping gardener's house. He likes to take paths instead of roads. He has an affinity with wild places. It comes from having had a jungle for a backyard when he was a boy. It comes from being left for days in a swamp during his army service. There is something more to why he leaves this way, avoiding the street. He hears the voice of the spirit Zulkanyan in his head. 'Go find your mother's stolen purse under the beast.'

The clouds are thick and thin across the moon. Sometimes there is a smattering of light, but it makes no difference because he can find his way in the dark. And even if he couldn't, he'd smell the thief from ten metres away. The decay of the man's dry breath snorts out like the stench of a rubber factory; the odour Kifli recognizes from the back of his mother's shoulder a few days earlier, as unique as a fingerprint.

Kifli slows down to a crawling pace, barely bending a blade of grass. Let the thief die in his sleep. It's easier.

He takes the almost weightless kris knife from behind his back where it is tucked into his pants, hidden under his shirt, and extracts the iron blade from its wooden sheath by pulling up on the hilt. Raises the point of the blade to his forehead, a sign of respect. A blade that was forged over seven years by an *empu* of good reputation, who fasted regularly and was known to infuse the many layers of metal with supernatural qualities while it was red-hot.

Kifli's incantations run silently through his head as familiar as a schoolboy's pledge. Still, he could kill the thief with a *pukul mati*, a Silat death strike to the base of the skull. He knows even before he begins there will be no contest. No fight. No defence. Certainly he will not do the killing; it is the knife that holds credit for all life it takes. The spirit Zulkanyan will be responsible for the physical blows. Somewhere between the blade and the spirit, Kifli Talib is a dim echo of a man who cannot distinguish himself from the others who occupy him.

Kifli passes under the bridge, a basket handle spanning the landscape. A deep breath as he goes. And another. And another. The voice in his head takes over. Zulkanyan, the spirit who has been with him almost since birth.

As Kifli relaxes, he is thinking about Rachel. His thoughts move to the image of his mother crying at the front door, twenty dollars for the market snatched up with her Koran in her purse. Then the picture fades. A dream is in its place. Kifli's mother and Rachel are walking down a road while gold fragments fall from the sky.

The hungry kris shakes in his hand as he steps closer.

When Kifli wakes up he is straddling a dead man.

The voice he hears says, 'Cut off the ears.'

With two fingers he prods the ears into the dirt until the boneless flesh is buried.

On the other side of the hill Kifli steps back onto the

street. The serpentine blade sleeping in its sheath under his shirt has been scraped in the dirt, red-brown.

By smelling so guilty, the thief had put himself on trial. His odour is less offensive now. The air will stay in his lungs and cool itself into salty gases that will eat his lungs away.

'Don't be so proud of yourself,' the spirit Zulkanyan says to Kifli. 'I found him for you.'

THE AW BROTHERS OF RENOWNED Tiger Balm fame had constructed a park to the Chinese Ten Gates of Hell. A dragon looming over the highway. Its long tail flowing like ribbons of sea waves. Inside the dragon's dismal belly, punishment for sins committed. This is where he takes her on his day off, to Haw Par Villa, a failing tourist attraction where there were few visitors, the spirit Zulkanyan telling him to test Rachel out. 'See what she knows and what she likes.' When Rachel had one leg out the taxi door she said, 'It's so hot, maybe we shouldn't go.' A kiddie sideshow surrounded the colossal dragon, beginning with giant fibreglass goldfish that dispensed food for the real fish in the ponds. The old man who sold Kifli admission tickets was also the refreshments vendor, the five-dollar astrologer, the postcard salesman, the bathroom attendant and the spirit tamer. Having lots of time to account for as the place was mostly forgotten, he was also part-time groundskeeper.

As Kifli&Rachel approached the dragon's mouth the spirit Zulkanyan said to Kifli, 'It is she who wants to see it all. If we scare her, she will get closer to us, closer to you.'

As they moved into the dragon's interior, two armed and

erect beasts, one with the head of an ox, the other a horse's face, were escorting disembodied souls into the Ten Gates of Hell. Rachel was sure she had a sudden fever. In the dark, it was hard for her to breathe. Yet here was something pleasant for her, it was cool inside—which made the place seem all the more bizarre in contrast to the sweltering heat outside. Incense smoke crowded the air, cruel deities squeezed the humidity into vaporous steam. Clusters of heads were moaning on a table, snakes slithered through their missing eyes. It seemed to Rachel that they were grabbing for her but that was impossible; their bodies were halfway down the river.

Each of the ten courts had its own king who oversaw the administration of punishment for sins committed on this mortal plane. In the third court King Songdi made sure drug traffickers were tied to a red-hot copper pillar and grilled.

In the dim sanctity of the inner pavilions, bodies were ground between stones, dismembered and disembowelled, then burned or frozen. Ghoulish fiends pulled out tongues and fried them in boiling oil.

The sixth court of hell was punishment for pornography, cheating, food wasting and misuse of books. Offenders were thrown onto a tree of knives. Others were drowning in blood, sliced in half, left to bleed like pomegranate seeds floating in scarlet juices.

Kifli led Rachel along. 'It's only plaster and paint.' Something that was hard not to notice as colours were fading and in some places chipped paint revealed chicken wire. He stuck his finger inside a tortured mouth, pushing his knuckles halfway down its throat. Warning the other spirits who had descended on Rachel from the moment she stepped out of the taxi to back off—she was already called for, she was only there for testing.

By the time Kifli confronted the rowdy entities, Rachel was dizzy and half-asleep, flashing strobe lights confused her as to which way to go. The special effects didn't help: creaking bridges, caves, ethereal tortures.

Her mind was on the rack.

Skeletons clutched and swung from the edges of a square that was closing in on her. Monsters' shadows crawled out of the coloured lights of the ice pond under the bridge she was crossing. She turned from those twisted faces to Kifli's. 'You said we were going to a Chinese garden.'

'That's what it's called.'

'But it's not. Not at all.'

'This is a garden of the Chinese underworld,' he said.

'It's evil,' she said. Then reluctantly, because she really liked him, 'No offence, Kifli, but who takes a woman to a torture chamber for a date?'

He wanted to tell her it wasn't his idea, he had to do it, and it would have been worse if he hadn't fended off the hungry spirits. Instead he led her past the pavilion of forgetfulness, where a wax figure of the old woman Meng Po administered tea from the cup of forgetting.

Kifli put his arm around Rachel's shoulders. She slanted into his long bone ribs. Outside, they stood against the dragon's tail while their eyes adjusted to the light. There was a rat with a gun and a cat with a camera. Giant grasshoppers, dressed in suits and ties, kissed.

Kifli propped Rachel against the front gate and waved for the taxi. She was as heavy as a dead body. Her voice had hardly any force. 'Why did we come here, Kifli? I don't believe in hell.' He pushed his groin into hers, his chest to her shoulders to keep her upright, his lips to her ear. 'Yes, you do,' he said. 'That's why you're here.'

And then on the way home in the taxi, she asked him if he ate popcorn at the movies. As if that were the defining cultural question and spirits were an altogether different issue. She swayed from one reality to another. Probably, Kifli thought, like they switch television channels in Canada. Kifli was confused. He saw her as a threat and a temptation. His whole life he'd been in a state of constant emotional restraint. To his friends, excessive passion was a form of disease. Like in Western movies, he had the notion that he was lovestruck. And Western movies always had happy endings.

Kifli saw her soft. He saw her lost. He saw her quivering lips. She was barely walking; he had to infuse her with his energy to get her from the taxi to her hotel room. He watched her sleeping from the end of her bed, until she rose through the porous stone that pressed into her chest every morning, with the sweet taste of sleeping potion, blue as a fairy blue-bird on her lips.

One of her arms hung over the edge of the bed. Silver, thick as a python, shifted down her wrist.

When she opened her eyes she saw him and smiled. 'I was afraid of the dark,' she said, 'when I was a little girl. Something was watching me from my closet. My sister, Dana, was afraid that someone would break into our house. I was never afraid of that, I was scared of the shadow that was always watching me. My father used to take me through every room and open all the closets. "See? There's no one in there." He didn't understand that whatever it was would never show itself when he was there. As soon as my father left the room it crept back in. Every night my father sat on my bed until I fell asleep. Sometimes he would rock me in the rocking chair. A few times I saw him leaving while I was still awake and he had to come back. Right now it seems like I've been away from home for a long time.'

Kifli took Rachel's hand, turned it over and began to read it. 'You're lonely.' Rachel's palm rose up a knowing into her head. From now on, I won't die for love. From now on, my heart will be protected by a cage with slim openings between the bars. From now on, when the little chicks die, I won't look at them. I won't mourn every squirrel eaten by the barn dog.

'Everyone is lonely, Kifli. Any soothsayer on any corner could tell me that.'

'You think your mother doesn't love you. It's not true.'

'What's true?'

'You will always want to travel, but your soul cannot stay anywhere but near to your father. And the sea took away your desire to record in your journal.'

'Anything else?' she said.

'I knew you were coming before we met.'

'Really? Who are you?' she said, which made him wonder if she knew.

'You want to know everything,' he said.

'Is that in my hand too?'

'No. All over you.'

'Maybe I knew about you too,' she said. 'From a dream.'

His lips were blackish. She wondered what they tasted like. 'Look at your hand,' she said. 'What does that mean?'

Kifli put his hand behind his back. Then he slowly brought it back around. 'This line that cuts straight across the middle. It's not so common. My guru says it means I have a talent for the spiritual aspect of Silat. I'm only allowed to study seven of the ten levels because I have the ability to do harm.'

'What kind of harm?'

'I don't know...maybe I could kill someone. Maybe I could do it without using physical strength. I studied further anyway, *ilmu ghaib*, concerning invisibility.'

'Maybe you're my teacher,' she said. As if he hadn't said murder.

'I'm the one who needs to learn,' he said.

'But you have a guru.'

'I have Silat. It's not for Westerners. It takes up so much time, so much prayer. I don't even have time to watch TV.'

'Who wants to do that?' she said. He takes her hand up again. 'I can tell you something else, you should say your prayers. God will protect you.' She doesn't know how dull it can be, dreary and suffocating, this reading people like he had already read the book.

She thinks she has never been so safe. Fire lurches inside her. 'I have you, Kifli, with a sword across your hand.'

*He is the puppet wolf, she is Red Riding Hood.*

He has been stirring his fingers around her palm, stirring up everything. When he touches her, the most forbidden, he feels blood swelling in his hands. His eyes are closed and rolling. He never would have dared to even sit on her bed without Zulkanyan prodding, 'She won't resist, take her.' Kifli knows the rest of the message without having to hear it—*take her or else.*

Kifli presses her spirit's door, the *shenmen* point of her heart line, in the small hollow at the crease in her wrist. To clear her channels and pacify her heart. To ground her absent-mindedness—her excessive dreaming.

And then, by the nature of love, it all becomes a dreamy-dream anyway.

This time, when he kisses her, the kiss is full of salt.

She cannot distinguish between her body's ramblings and his hands. A single flow of blood. She wanders sleepily around his body. His slim waist. The longness of his legs. The emptiness of his belly. He goes on so long, without ending, she thinks he is keeping his soul away from her. He is used to waiting, having fasted for thirty days before his first vision. Half of him is in the realm of her creation, the other with the spirit Zulkanyan, who whispers into his head, 'Put your hand here, your mouth there.' The spirit is the one who knows what her body wants. Kifli is lost in the terrible calculated afternoon.

She needs to eliminate any distractions from the man-boy: his dreams, his secret Silat training, his Guru. His future. A hiss from his mouth, a tepid jet of pheromones from his skin. *He is mine.*

When Kifli finally comes inside Rachel, a thrust of hormones flood along the lining of his heart. His skin receptors kick his brain into a spontaneous attempt to expel the spirit. Zulkanyan withstands the brief charge. Kifli has to be some kind of man sometime. Ecstasy bursts in his brain. Then he is compelled to pull Rachel closer and sleep safely buried under her, a blue-grey cast off heavy warm flesh, their feet tangled, his hands sleeping in her hair. He spoons her into the curve of him. When he wakes up full of conflict, he imagines the hotel room as their matrimonial home and Rachel as his wife.

Kifli is sleeping on his back. His arm under her neck. He doesn't tell her he was a virgin until they have slept into the evening, when he wakes in a state of remorse. He says he had the same fear at fifteen, when he was paraded through the kampong moments before his circumcision. She wonders how at nearly thirty, a man could be so underwritten.

He paces the floor. 'This isn't how it's supposed to be. I didn't want to. Forgive me, I raped you.' She says she wanted to do it. 'No,' he says. 'You've been away from home. You don't know what you want. Forgive me, I've made you unclean.'

She hears shower water. Sees steam from under the bathroom door. He comes out wrapped in a towel and slouches at the end of the bed, shoulders heaving. It is half an hour before he inches up the bed and lies beside her.

He has decided to tell everyone. When the whole family is sitting down to supper he will announce his affair with the Jewess, saying she is beautiful, not a monster, and that he has the same love for her as for his mother, who is second after God. After that he will escape from his unbearable shame to a black corner. Zulkanyan will pick up the fork from the plate and feed him. Zulkanyan will tell the mother she has a filthy boy who could kill her in her sleep.

He no longer felt he was the same as everybody else, always at the subway on time, making his way to work, being obsessively polite and genuinely helpful. Kifli now imagined himself as a spy for the underworld, not the spirit world—the world of secret love. Pleasure. Breaking the law. He was a fugitive, sitting in the dentist chair with a frozen mouth and two new fillings. A place that until that very moment made him feel inferior. Since he was loving Rachel, his Chinese dentist was just another bloke, and he was no longer like everyone, or maybe he thought, on his way to meet her, he was now exactly like a man and had never known that before.

He stood on the concrete floor of the alcove outside Dragon City Shopping Arcade, jelly-legged, pulling one foot up and then the other, back and forth as if lifting his feet out of mud. He was always at their meeting places ahead of her, waiting patiently in slowtime. He had to be careful what he said to Rachel about her condition, her sleeping and difficult breathing. In the state she was in, it would be confusing for her to have to memorize so many foreign words. It was better for Kifli to use simple terms that she could understand. Words like soul, which was void of specific aspects and qualities—words like spirit and guru. Words like God.

Love makes stories move fast. It tells us so much about who we are whether we want it to or not. Love makes us transparent. All Kifli wanted was to get back to the arms he loved.

Rachel lifted her dress up over her head in the bathroom—took off her panties and unclasped her bra in a hurry at the side of the bed. Kifli held his arms up like he was going to catch her falling from the sky, like he was praying, like she was a roof of glass.

'Once a man was sent from Indonesia to Canada to bring the wandering spirit Zulkanyan home. Before he could accomplish his task, the venomous jets of a dark cobra snake, to which there is no cure, sprayed him.' Kifli brought stories of incantations and revenge, from not so far away in the jungle. He spoke legends from his eyes, and out of his mouth a string of words that he will both contradict and confirm so eventually Rachel won't know what he has ever said. Kifli's tales sounded like the Brothers Grimm fables Rachel used to read before bed, under her sheets with a flashlight while she was waiting for her father. Nothing more devious than a wolf disguised as a grandmother. Teeth, all the better to eat you with. Kifli began with the guru and the Silat martial art. He sowed the idea in Rachel's head that he had acquired powers through discipline and devotion. He lied to her about Zulkanyan and instead described Qadar, the priest who had led an uprising against Dutch invaders in Java and was finally destroyed when his limbs were amputated and buried five miles apart in opposite directions from the trunk of his body. Qadar died a hero, pointing to the east, the west, the north, the south, like a broken compass. No other deed could kill him. A priest who was for many years committed to silence, Qadar was loved by everyone in the kampong, and immune to weapons of all kinds except the metal gold. When a traitor told the invading marauders that a gold bullet could kill him, the priest was promptly assassinated. Soon after, a poisonous spider bit the traitor, driving him mad. He ran around the kampong confessing, 'I forged the gold. I killed the beloved man who sent my mother's spirit to God.' He was found in the jungle with his throat slit by a machete.

When Kifli Talib told Rachel his fantastic stories they clung to her like the millions of flying fox bats hanging upside down from the mangrove trees at night. Rachel, wide-eyed and full of fever, was hungry for all of it.

Kifli's mother saw him and began to cry. 'What's happening to you?'

'Nothing you want to know about, mother.'

'Let's go to the guru.'

'I have already been. I know something you don't want me to know, and I'm happy about it.'

'You have *sakit cinta*, the love sickness is talking to your mother. You're not here. When your father comes home we'll go to the guru.'

Kifli's sister was watching *Hawaii Five-O*, crying too. She was a spinster. She had a good job. Kifli said, 'Do you want me to be like her? An *anak dara tua*. It would be better if she married a stranger.'

'Shh, the neighbours...,' his mother said.

'The neighbours,' he said. 'I didn't get the blessing for Tina. I didn't marry her. I didn't do anything about that. We were stupid. I should have fought for her.' His head was buzzing with rejection after the request so hopefully delivered to his expected bride's parents' home was turned down.

*Mr. and Mrs. Talib send their best wishes, the height of which the mountains are comparatively low. They desire to pick a flower from your garden for their son to wear as a posy.* Now that he was thinking about it, it must have been Zulkanyan who formed the reply in Tina's parents' heads. *The flower in our garden is still a bud and therefore not suitable for a posy.*

SHE IS SLEEPING IN THE GARDEN of the Palm Court. He raises her feet from the chair without waking her and slides himself under her heels. He has been told by Zulkanyan to take a lock of her hair. 'Don't push me,' Kifli says to the spirit. 'She is mine too.' He is shocked by his rebellion; knowing there will be punishment soon, he adds, 'I'll tell her more of Qadar's story. What a martyr she'll think you were.'

She speaks to him even before opening her eyes. 'Have you finished your shift?'

'Yes. Do you want to go to the room?'

'Someone might see you.'

'I don't care.'

'What's wrong?'

'Nothing.'

'Maybe it's going to rain.'

'No.'

'Maybe I'm still sick.'

'*Sayang,*' he says, 'I love you, *Cinta, Sayang.*'

'I love you too.'

'I saw my guru.'

'Why didn't you take me?'

'He wants me to help you.'

'Why, what's wrong?'

'You're tired again, aren't you?'

'Do you want to go to the room and sleep? I could do that.'

'The guru said spirits are eating your energy.'

'How does he know?'

'He can see.'

'How?'

'He can feel. I don't question him.'

She rolls her eyes.

'Come on, Rachel, what are you doing here? You don't act like a tourist.'

'I'm sick.'

'You're full of spirits.'

'So what if I am?'

'One of your spirits is an ancestor of mine. I need to send it where it belongs. It doesn't belong here.'

She's very sleepy again.

'They're fighting me right now,' he said. 'Let me do a cleansing before you leave. I'll send the spirit to face the other world. It doesn't want to go. It recognized me right away, through your eyes.'

'There's something there, Kifli, but I don't know what.'

'I made love to you. You made me believe it was right. Let me help you.'

'Fine,' she said. 'Take your spirit.'

WORSE THAN A MULTITUDE OF GHOSTS, there were unmanageable destructive ramblings in her head. There was no going back into her history for help; her ancestors were either burned out of Russian documents or frighteningly unstable. Rachel nurtured the insidious voice that came into her head because she hardly ever heard a different one. It came into her head every time she couldn't answer the flash card, 8 x 8, or 7 x 6, and when she couldn't tell left from right until she was eleven, when she still had to close her eyes to find her writing hand. Nana taught her that trick.

It was her own internal narrative that made her feel worthless. *What makes you think you can do that? No. There you go, making a fool of yourself again. Ugly girl. Not worth loving.* There was a lot to take out of her whether she had a spirit or not. Truckloads that she couldn't get rid of. So let the magician Kifli do it. Maybe he would replace the voice that haunted her with blue sky, or soft motherly hands.

If Kifli could make things disappear she'd give away the things that hurt her: mean words, lies, Pink Bunny's death, the fog in her head that made people call her flaky, abandonment, her family's inability to communicate, leaving her feeling locked in a room, unable to understand them. 'They don't get me, Nana.' She'd give away the deep void inside, her emotional isolation; the fear that life might end before she woke up, that she didn't know anyone in the obituaries and now they were dead; the body count during the Vietnam War that came up on the six o'clock news right after *Commander Tom* and *Batman*; the picture in *Life* magazine of a sixteen-year-old dead girl sprawled across a set of stairs from an overdose of mescaline; the camps, the trains, the turning of heads.

She wanted to surrender but she couldn't—it wasn't safe. Maybe with a magician in Singapore she could spit out the thing that haunted her most.

That love was not forever.

She believed it was living spirits that possessed her: Lynton, her father, her teachers. Her own defeat. Who had time to worry about the others. The farmer Garnet Warren, she thought, being the most quiet and harmless of them all. He was utterly gorgeous in the way he made himself known. Making weeping willows dance and then rest, like heaven. So without God, or making do with the one at hand, Rachel gave herself over to Kifli, begging him to rescue her.

*Take it out.*

*I am possessed.*

The thing that scared her the most. The feeling that stability was always just beyond her reach, and everyone knew it. Maybe no one could help her. So why not go over to the woods like the white British Raja of Sarawak did next door in Borneo? Have you ever seen a shrunken head? Wondered what it would be like to be one hanging under a longhouse, or where dreams come from, or where our brains go after a couple of hours in front of the television.

*I want to rid my life of fear—of time sifting through sleep.*

The world of a Malay magician is the breadth of a tray with a sky, the breadth of an umbrella.

Is it, she wonders, that I want to be you, Kifli? Or am I already a part of you and that which knows, cries to join in, with symbols and drums, in layers of skirts—food offerings, in the heat and in the smoke, without form or conscience, or hair of any kind. Without attachment. No knowledge of the past or future. Only the finest ripples on the water so you will know I am here. Maybe I am you and you already sense it. I'm willing to go anyplace for help. Anyplace is a place I could never find at home.

THERE IS A GRAVEYARD SET in a shallow valley at the junction of Beach and Java roads, tree barks as grey and sullen as the tombstones set on blue clay, untouched by the typhoons of the China Sea or Bay of Bengal. In the monotonous heat she followed Kifli criss-cross through the graves so she wouldn't step on bones, on a stretch of grass that was once forest. 'Usually for *mandi bunga* we use coconuts and flowers,' he said. 'We need something stronger to fight the dark sickness in you, Rachel Lynn Gold. We need help from dead souls.'

He didn't have to pry at her at all, which made him think she was easy to take, but then—she could be a trap.

'Come on,' he said. 'Pick some.' She held on to the back of his shirt. If anything grabbed at her ankles, she could jump up into his arms. 'We should have washed our hands,' she said.

'Rachel, please pick something more.'

'My shoes are getting wet.' Catherine's prayer emerged.

*Af-Bri is the name of the angel of rain designated to form and thicken clouds, to empty them and to cause water to fall.*

'Rachel, please.'

'These are new shoes.'

'Don't look at me like that.'

'Like what?'

'Nothing. Forget it.'

'I'm doing this for you,' she said. But it wasn't true.

They traipsed over the shelly layers of earth where the Pacific plate and the Indian Ocean plate collide. An island that had more than one hundred and fifty thunderstorms a year, where almost every living thing was pretending to be something else, waiting with the patience of Job for prey: a forest spider resting on a palm leaf, disguised as a white feather, stick insects, leaf bugs, orchid mantises—all as inert as the bodies below.

Kifli picked plants from around the black headstones. 'We have to fight.' *Kur Allah*, he said to himself. *Cluck, cluck, God.*

He needed the mid-rib of the leaves of forty plants that lay near the graves: *Ficus, Myrtus, Passiflora. Sea ghosts drink the soul.* He grabbed handfuls while Rachel plucked one leaf at a time from higher stems. She rubbed their skin and put them to her nose.

'Does this place seem familiar to you?' Kifli said.

'Familiar?'

A wild shiver ran through her. Froze her. Kifli dropped his pickings, the plants falling in a bundle at Rachel's feet like the swish of a farmer's sheaf. He pulled her close to him. Kifli saw long digits of a grey hand hanging over her back. You're not real, he assured himself, whoever you are. He rubbed Rachel's arms and kissed her forehead. 'There's a cold spot here,' she said. 'Do you feel it?'

'Where?'

'Right here, where we're standing.'

'Are you afraid?'

'Are you?'

'Do you like it here?'

'Here? Why would I like it?'

'But you agreed.'

Kifli rested his chin on her shoulder and took a deep breath. 'I've never done this by myself,' he said.

'Don't do it then.' She said. 'Don't you want to?'

'I have to. I can't let you continue like this.'

He bent down, scooped up the plants that had fallen, took Rachel's hand and ran to the street. The house of the dead retreated into dense silence. Bamboo rats and pencil-tailed tree mice scurried out of holes for food under threat of flat-headed bats.

The spirit Zulkanyan was giddy with passion. 'Sing her an *ilmu pengasih*. A love spell. I hear your prayers under the curses; they won't do you any good.'

The further they ran from the cemetery, the more disappointed Rachel felt. It was all exciting when Kifli said she had a spirit; the way he flitted around the graveyard made her wonder if he had any idea what he was doing. He acted as if there was someone else with them, but there were just sleeping hornbills and barbets and leaf birds in the trees.

Rachel had always had a buffer between her and unwanted danger. A plump pillow of protection. It came from me and from her father, who tried to stand in the way of everything that might cause her pain, inciting instead an extraordinary amount of grief. This sense of safety allowed Rachel to float. How was she to land? What was there to hold her to the earth? Her self-actualizing, swamis, Chinese Gods, Buddha, meditation, commiseration. Even Lord George

Gordon Byron distracted her from being grounded. Once, after reading a biography of Houdini, she held a séance to communicate with Byron, woke up in the middle of the night beating on Lynton. 'Open the door and let them in.'

She loved being a foreigner. All of it was awash over her. Having never seen before, never been before, except in her dreams, she was part of the mountain above the valley, part of the road piled with rotting durian peels and garbage. She was the curiosity of her whitish presence in a faraway place. At least as a foreigner she thought she could be herself. Whatever that is. How should she know? At home, she felt there was no value to intuitive knowledge. Feeling didn't answer exam questions or provide a career, as far as she knew there were no openings for a seat at the oracle at Delphi. So what else could she do but observe the mystical presences in her life?

No home. No map. No road. No way, ticket, passport, no difference between the sky and the underground and the dimension she lived in. For a long time she wondered what was wrong with the others, until they made her wonder what was wrong with her.

Raffles Hotel was impressive that night. A moon at the end of the drive. White pillars suggested the luxury of space. Men in white uniforms and turbans mingled around the front entrance. The rest of the place was dead quiet. The air was dense when Rachel and Kifli entered room 107. The plants in Kifli's hand covering the straight line that crossed his palm.

He undressed her while the bathwater ran. His hands were cold. When he put her in the bath, she jumped. The water too was cold. Tearing the leaves off the stems he placed them around her. They floated on the surface of the water. He knew that water weakens boundaries.

Rachel was laughing. This was a game she could play with him.

'You should have been fasting,' Kifli said. 'You should be pure, but we don't have time.' All his broken rules meant nothing to her, but Kifli was getting increasingly frantic. The plants knocked against Rachel's skin. Kifli put his hands around her head. His whole body vibrated like an electric wave. Her head shook too, as if she had been waiting so long for that moment. Rachel released a huge sigh. 'I'm never going home.' His rituals gave her a sense of order in a world she never made. She had her own superstitious practices. Before field hockey games, Rachel listened to Bob Marley's 'Exodus' while she wrapped her ankles, then tied her lucky red string around her hockey stick. She had to be alone and she had to tie her shoes before the end of the song, or her team would lose the game. She also had to wear Lynton's family ring around her neck and tuck a lucky rock into her jacket pocket. She took lucky rocks to exams too, laid four of them out on the table before she began. She had to write tests with her lucky pen, but in fact Rachel's marks improved only after her mother told her that everything she ever read was stored firmly in her brain; it was only a matter of relaxing enough to retrieve the information.

If she wanted Lynton to call, she read a book. For her

mother's attention, she slammed doors. When she wanted love, she denied it.

The one thing she never did was pray.

She cried a lot instead.

Kifli stirred Rachel into the bath of leaves with inaudible prayers. When Rachel said she'd had enough, she was going to climb out, Zulkanyan's order to take her overcame him. 'Wait,' he said.

Kifli turned over the leaves, setting the spell.

A blessing became a curse. Death would begin with the weakening of Rachel's soul. Kifli could take her right away but then she would no longer be his, she would be Zulkanyan's.

Kifli was making heavy sounds, like the ones used for old magical operations requiring:

*Tongues of secretly exhumed stillborn babies*
*The blood of a murdered man*
*One's own blood*
*The oil of a green coconut*
*One's own shadow*

All they had were leaves.

His arms lifted her out and he laid her on the bed over a white hotel towel; Rachel assumed in case she bled, maybe from her mouth or ears, if what she had to expel came rushing out.

Kifli fell unconscious on the bed next to her.

He tried to sit up, then fell back down. Eventually, after a few attempts, he was able to stand, walk into the bathroom

and spit a black ball of blood into the sink. He came out stag-
gering over to her.

His hands moved in circles around her belly—shaking
like a lightning rod that had been struck.

'I don't feel anything,' Rachel said. 'Nothing's happening.'
Cold and shivering she laughed. 'How come something's happening to you and I feel exactly the same?'

'Shh, he's here.'

Kifli's head flung forward. Zulkanyan flooded in. A
deep breath in…a deep breath out…in, *satu-dua-tiga-
empat-lima-enam-tujuh-lapan-sembilan-sepuluh*. Birds smash
themselves into windows and stun themselves into simu-
lated death.

She didn't know how a spirit could have penetrated the
man-boy—maybe a puff of smoke in through his nose or a
shift in energies that altered Kifli's humours, making him
briefly punch-drunk, until the spirit entered. By the time Kifli
was blinking and the corners of his mouth sagged, the
changeover was complete. Lifting his head regally, twisting
his neck and shoulders slightly as if adjusting to the host
body, the spirit grunted a stream of small mammal snorts.

By then Rachel's face was close to his, the cadence of his
sleight of mind travelling miles into her.

His eyes flew open.

Nothing had changed in the air. But Kifli's voice wasn't
his own. 'Do not touch her,' the spirit said. 'My name is
Zulkanyan and I will destroy you. My name is Zulkanyan.'

'What's going on?' she cried.

Zulkanyan spoke to her. 'My child, I have been with Kifli
for a long time. I am the one who is helping you. I will take
your spirit away. I will tell Kifli what to do and I will take care

of this for you. There are three of them in there, one woman who has killed someone, there is a man...'

'I don't like this anymore, Kifli. I don't like this. You're acting strange.' She desperately pushed the man-boy's back.

Zulkanyan didn't flinch. 'Don't you want to know who they are?'

'No, I don't. Just wake up. Wake up.'

How long will it take to get to the door? How much money was left? How many times had she worn her jeans before washing them? Days before the next city? Hours before dinner? Seconds before the hot water ran out?

Rachel was flat out on the bed, her soul defended by the resounding hymn from Catherine and what amulets and symbols her eyes had gathered in from Jerusalem, Egypt and Kathmandu. The rest of her was paralyzed with fear and fascination.

Zulkanyan felt her pulse. 'Your heart's beating too fast. You're frightened, I should go.'

'Don't go,' she said. 'Don't go.' Adrenalin made her short of breath. 'Do you mind if I have a cigarette?'

'Smoke if you want to. It's your world,' said the spirit.

When she sucked on the smoke, grains of gold tobacco exploded. At that moment nothing was ever so vivid or colours so clear and vibrant. Outside the room everything was black. The spirit's voice was seething with compassion as he spoke of God—to whom Rachel trusted he was closely connected.

The girl was as lucid as an astronaut.

*Lift my burden. Give me a sign that we are coded from heaven.*

She wanted miracles no matter how she got them.

THE *BOMOH* SAID, 'I will call to this spirit, and it will be named Zulkanyan, protecting Kifli until he is strong enough to be on his own.' That was the agreement, Kifli said to Rachel. But Zulkanyan never left. My parents are from Java. Grandfather also from Java. I was one or two years old and sick with a high fever. Western doctors were expensive and hard to come by. They were Christians so we stayed away from them. We had mediums in the kampong. My grandfather brought me to this old man who said, 'Bring fruit for the spirits to eat. Bring this, bring that. Sacrifice chickens.' Glutinous yellow rice is a beautiful colour for spirits. It's their favourite food, like champagne for a wedding.

Then the old *bomoh* cut off the end of a lime where it had been pulled from the branch. If it turned over in a bowl of water, the baby was very sick, otherwise it was a common illness. When he cut the lime he said, 'If you hadn't come to me, this boy would have died. This will cost you more than just food. You have to bring down a goat.' So grandfather bought a goat and sacrificed it. The medium said, 'I'm going to call a spirit, to save his soul.' Zulkanyan was linked to me for protection.

Before the Muslims came the people here worshipped anything that came along. We are Malays, not Arabs. We still feel that spirits are everywhere. To add Mohammed wasn't too much trouble.

My family came to Singapore when I was seven. My father sailed in an Indonesian boat. He was never at home. I went to school, but I didn't have any friends. I could make a baby cry from very far away. Bullies wouldn't come near me. One stare would scare them. And that's when I knew it wasn't me who was looking at them. It was Zulkanyan.

I can see death, like the way I saw you in a vision before you came. Hey, look, this man will die. True enough, he died. I did that a few times and people were afraid of me.

Out of the many students my guru has, I was the only one he called for trance healing. But all I have to do is exist. I don't do anything myself. The guru holds my hand and tries to get Zulkanyan to appear. Sometimes he sweats for a long time. Sometimes Zulkanyan won't come.

I never cared about what I did. It was my job, and Zulkanyan has always protected me. He orders me around. 'Pick the plants,' so I pick them. Zulkanyan says that you will belong to us. I think he means you will belong to him. That's why he said, 'Make her pick too.'

SINCE HIS FIRST APPEARANCE, Zulkanyan spoke to Rachel every day. He took over Kifli whenever he wanted to. Kifli was a vehicle with amenities—language and mobility.

Rachel shivered as if she were out in the Toronto winter, in the damn monsoon heat. Her teeth could chatter for an hour. She kept the promise she'd made not to tell Kifli about her conversations with Zulkanyan. He said Kifli would be angry. Kifli had to fast for many days before his first vision and would not appreciate Rachel's instant success in communicating with the spirit.

Meeting up with a spirit was kind of like going to a rock concert at Maple Leaf Gardens in Toronto. Police at every entrance. Some with dogs. The plainclothes ones were further back, mixing in the crowd but still noticeable. Rachel had been searched by security at Jethro Tull and Queen; she didn't have any drugs on her, but they rummaged through her purse anyway.

The scalpers in front of Maple Leaf Gardens, are you a cop or just a guy who wants tickets? Are you a good witch or a bad witch? Tickets for Johnny Winter, hockey tickets for tonight, on the glass.

First a scalper tucked his tickets under his jean jacket. 'Cop?' 'No way. I need a pair of golds.' Out came the merchandise.

Who knew who anyone really was and what judgment or authority was going to reign down on her?

Zulkanyan spoke about Kifli as if he were a hopeless boy, when really he was a hopeless man who had recently become very hopeful.

'My child...' Zulkanyan always began with an address. He considered himself a holy shrine, riddler that he was. 'Believe in God.'

'Yes, but who built the pyramids?' Rachel said.

'You're asking me that again?'

Zulkanyan never answered any of her questions about history or other worlds; he gave nothing that she couldn't read in a book. But when he blew on her bangle and turned it white, he broke the laws of science.

Where was she going to put this information from the tree of knowledge?

'Yes,' she said. 'But why six million? What happened to Hitler's soul?'

'Transition,' was his only answer. Something about reincarnation and the absence of punishment. The spirit couldn't imagine punishment for Hitler's soul—but for Kifli it was a perpetual threat. If the Malay man-boy didn't do what he was told, he would be bumped down a flight of stairs or be imprisoned for hours in the elevator at his parents' apartment building.

Rachel fearfully grabbed Kifli as soon as he returned to his body. Terror was part of the entertainment. Like being stoned at a concert. Now she was straight and feeling like she had dropped acid. A tree is pliable. A glass is liquid. A stone is sand. In a hole in the wall behind Rachel's bedroom closet a spaceship launched at night. Anyone who has ever done shrooms knows reality is expandable.

IN FRONT OF THE VANITY MIRROR in the bathroom Rachel held Kifli's face and they looked at his reflection, staring without blinking at the edge of the dark cusps where the acid had burnt his cheeks, until the imperfections were bursting out at them.

'I think you're fine the way you are,' she said.

'They're ugly.'

'I didn't even notice.'

'Then why do you keep looking at them?'

'They're spaces for my lover's water to fall into. So there. I love them.'

'Why do you say things like that?' he said. 'It makes it worse.' He would rather look at anything else. Look at her smooth brown eyes. 'Just do it.'

She split a bobby pin between her teeth and pinned back his bangs, then squeezed a line of zinc cream along her hand, her tongue resting on her upper lip. She filled the holes in his face. 'It's not going to work,' she said. 'You can't make scars disappear with cream. You look like a ghost.' He looked like a mask on a wall. Kifli tried to wipe the chalky paste off, but some of it wouldn't come out, so Rachel used the corners of a damp cloth. Kifli sat still on the edge of the bathtub while she melted the rest out with steaming towels.

He cried.

She laughed, grabbed her belly and rolled from side to side against the wall between the sink and the toilet. She told him to close his eyes, she was always telling him to close his eyes. 'Give me your hand. Do you feel that? My fat ass. My arms. I hate them. Dana has long slender arms.'

The white towel wrapped around her ears muffled their words into shapes, into tones, as if their words were coming from inside her head. She uncapped the jar of mud she had carried from the Dead Sea.

'In the desert we baked ourselves to detoxify our skin.'

She returned to the mirror and blackened her face.

'Do you see anything different about me when my eyes are all that's left?' He keeps staring. He sees an entirely different face, hissing and spitting at him. He sees her eyes filled with blood, not blinking, not looking at herself. Looking at him. Rachel might not even know. She's not responsible for what she looks like when her soul is resisting.

'At Ein Gedi, at a kibbutz by the Dead Sea,' she said. 'The mud protected me from the sun. I wasn't ashamed of my body when I wore it. I walked along the rim of *Yam Hamelach*, the Dead Sea, and because I wasn't self-conscious I reinterpreted everything. First my body; I was almost invisible, just an outline. All the effort it took to present myself to the world was gone. With the heavy minerals in my hair, sucking toxins out of my scalp, I became light-headed.'

What Kifli sees is her hair standing up on its end.

'Then the salt deposits looked like ice, and the orange trees like the sun. The mountain Massada was above us, where an entire population of Jews chose to commit suicide rather than be enslaved by the Romans, who had bored a hole in the fortress wall. When archaeologists uncovered the hidden village, they also discovered a *mikvah*. But how did the zealots get water for their holy bath? How did they carry it up from the Dead Sea without being seen? Maybe they only used rainwater like your coconut milk. Rain in the desert? I don't think so.

'I walked without shoes on the hot sand. German tourists posing in front of their cameras were covered in mud like me. I heard them laughing and joking, and for the first time in my life the German language sounded human. *Wieder Mazada failt nicht.*' She cupped her breasts in her hands. 'Cover me with mud, Kifli.'

He had good hands.

When he finished there were splatters of minerals on his face, his handprints were on Rachel's hips. She told him to take off his clothes so she could do him too.

She left his penis to stir against her stomach and thighs as she plastered him. There was a startling intensity in his breathing and in his natural ability to relax. Like a hallucination—a pre-sleep while reaching for him, she learned that bodies are musical and move in waves. *This soft leather in your hand, in your body-mouth, asleep at your hip, is my wedding vow.*

He had dents of haphazard shapes in his face. She had thick legs and hips.

He said she was the only one he wanted in this world.

She felt voluptuous.

The small space and predictable utilities of the bathroom softened their unhappiness. A bathtub. A sink. A toilet to use as a chair, also to pee in, while talking about the Prambabab meteorite in Java from which the palace *empu* forged mystical kris blades.

Water was trickling in the sink.

They were mud people.

'...And once Sir Thomas Stamford Raffles wanted to limit kris wearing to royalty. It was completely rejected. Imagine, asking everyone to run around naked. A Malay without his kris.'

'And yours,' she said tugging on his penis.

He couldn't say. At the time of his oath, his *bersumpah*, the juice of a green lime ate into his blade, staining his lips with rust. '*Jika aku belut, aku dimakan keris.* If I turn traitor, may I be consumed by this kris.'

Kifli watched Rachel study his face in the mirror. He longed for her—to simply be alone with her.

He sat on the toilet. Rachel climbed into his dry brittle branches. Into something they had made together—a new skin that reeked like cicada shells, drying, cracking in little frayed squares and rectangles, pulling on their skin underneath.

In the bathroom, white porcelain fixtures: a bath, a wash-basin, a white tiled floor and tiled walls. Mud stinging around her eyes and thin-skinned areas, including her lip membrane.

The lovers could have escaped to the bedroom. In a more spacious room, they would have a wider perspective. Neither of them touched the doorknob. Or looked at it. Or noticed. In a small room with hard surfaces Kifli&Rachel had a comprehensible universe, definable; water ran from a hidden pipe behind the wall into the bath, predictable; the toilet wouldn't melt into a dream.

Four walls for feet, hands, elbows, knees, heads, stomachs, asses, for sliding down and aligning to, a ceiling not so far up, a firm floor that is not for digging but for lying on cold tile, where they slept after his cum dropped from her like a spit-ball into the toilet.

Foggy fish-semen dried on her stomach.

After they slept on rolled-out towels on the bathroom floor, Kifli tried to wipe it off. She pushed his hands away.

The words he told her to repeat sounded like ancient poetry:

*Aku ialah aku*
*Kenali diri mu sendiri*
*Insya Allah*

*I am I*
*Who am I*
*I know who I am*
*It is God's will*

She would repeat anything he asked her to. His words made her feel free while hers seemed heavy and monotonous. She was flattered that Kifli would share secret incantations of Silat. And even I who knew what was behind Kifli couldn't tell how he really felt. He had so many people to please: his mother, his guru, Zulkanyan, Singaporean society. And opposing them, Rachel, whose words he wanted to recite. Her words were clear and crisp to him. She taught him the expression 'by the book,' which was how she viewed his lifestyle, the song 'The Itsy Bitsy Spider,' then proceeded to tell Kifli a traveller's story she was told. 'There are two British businessmen and a Nigerian on a voyage through the South China and Java seas. One of the Brits had travelled all through the East, while the other knew everything there was to know about the West. While they were listing places they had been in the most uninterested, mundane tone, the Nigerian couldn't help but overhear their conversation. He went over to the two Englishmen and said, "By any chance has either one of you ever had delirious malaria tremors?" "No," said one. "Never," said the other. "Well then," said the Nigerian, "you gentlemen have never been anywhere and you have never seen anything." Doesn't that just crack you up, Kifli? I love that one.'

Kifli believed he understood Rachel. Not her Jewishness or her inarticulate struggle to find herself or her quick moods, but her move into myth to cope.

'You think I'm so innocent?' he said.

'Yes, as a matter of fact.'

'Just because I don't comment on everything doesn't mean I'm stupid. At this hotel we keep secrets.' He stood up. 'I have had delirious tremors.'

SHE IS BEACHED OVER HIS BODY. Scars, tears and burns where he is blue and darker in flesh. Kifli's textured skin is sensitive to Rachel's investigation. He tries to roll over onto his stomach, to hide, but she holds his shoulders down saying he has to tell her everything now that she has unearthed him.

He tells her the stories of his maimed body. He speaks of such violence; it is incomprehensible to her, hard to piece together what he says with the man she knows.

Pausing her hands over his long back, Rachel fits her fingers into the welts, feeling her way, briefly stopping on each remote wound that dips into his history, rubbing the hollow of the scars with a salve of cool lavender. As it seeps into his skin the fragrance warms, rises to Rachel's nose, down her throat, so that flashes of purple blink behind her eyes when she swallows, her hands riding the yawning scars from his river crossing.

During army exercises Kifli was in the front line of the platoon and responsible for the others behind. It would be a disgrace if another unit ambushed them. In the jungle there was a subtle forgetfulness that overcame him. Half a mile in through the trees he couldn't be sure where he was; it was hard to get out without luck. That time, he was not a magician, was abandoned by the spirit when he was up to his neck in a swamp. Kifli's head bobbed down the river like a coconut. He waded through the murky water where no bridges could be constructed. His feet were on guard for a twig or branch that might take him under. The clips for his assault rifle, rocks in his pockets, his kit on his back, while bloodsuckers found their way under his shirt.

He needed the hot tip of an ember to burn the leeches off his skin. Across his back there are divots where the bloodsuckers fell back into the water half cooked from the burning cigarette. The fat ones full of Kifli's blood, often snuffing the heater. Another soldier had to get the ones he couldn't reach, and Kifli did the same for him.

Rachel heaps the cloudy marks of Kifli's skin into a long sentence, stringing the words together like something silver she would wear around her neck: grown over, webbed, dark crevices—tender above what Kifli had ever given attention to. His body disappears except for the marks that Rachel preserves by touching. How did he ever sleep with so many open wounds? 'And then, my God, you had to turn around and cross the river again before morning.'

Rachel imagined the Malay in the Singapore army as sleeping fish on the backs of dragons. Kifli crossing the river as a large carp covered in leeches, his red fleshy mouth open out of the water so he could breathe, a soldier without rank—whom no one would ever notice—washed up on the small piece of island, stranded in jungle fog while there was no war. Just little caves of flesh and darkness.

His strong, flexible limbs that were spontaneous instruments of the Silat martial art arrested her.

He lived through his body and often not in it.

Rachel returned to the pockmarks on his face. 'Are these from the leeches too?'

'No,' he cupped his hands over the rubble. 'From acid. My friend and I were chased by a Chinese gang. Someone threw a pail of acid off the back of a truck and it hit my face.'

'What did he do that for?'

'Chinese hate Malays.'

'But there must have been another reason.'

'Zulkanyan warned me. He said, "Cover your eyes."'

She touched his face.

'Do you trust me?' he said to her.

'Of course I do.'

'How much?'

'Why?'

'Promise you won't hate me if I tell you.'

'I promise.'

'I killed him.'

'Who?'

'The Chinese who did it.'

She didn't understand what he'd just said. She wore a smirk, as if she had done it herself. Not accepting his story she twisted it into a common boy brawl. 'What are you talking about?'

'I'm a murderer, Rachel.'

She looked at her hands. She twisted them around her silver wrists.

He wept until she took him into her arms, her bed, her mouth. It is an unbelievable confession.

'You killed him,' she said.

'Yes.'

She has never even seen the Malay man-boy scorn, not an ill-willed salutation to anyone. Even when he speaks of spirits, it's matter of fact, without any investment. She is his only investment.

'You must have had a good reason,' she said.

'Zulkanyan told me to.'

Her brain went drunk. It took a detour to the left and to the right at the same time. The wings of a ferry bluebird landed on her brain and flew away with it.

'Well, there you go. You were under orders, it's not even your fault.'

What did she just say? Was he crying? Was she a priest? Did she have to hear this confession? Was she a witness now? Six million murders in her history—plus one.

She heard the rest of the story with fish-semen crystals sleeping on her belly. He said, 'There were twelve. Three of them in revenge. The other nine...I don't remember. I killed them in my sleep. Zulkanyan led the way. The man who stole my mother's purse. I could smell his blood under her fingernails. I killed him too.'

No matter what Kifli told her, she would decide for herself what was believable about him. There were codes of conduct in Asia that had nothing to do with her. 'You're not going to scare me away,' she said.

He was her virgin.

'He came to me,' she said.

'Who?' His body shuddered when he understood it was Zulkanyan. Then the knowing rose up into his eyes.

'No, that's not possible.'

'He told me not to tell you.'

'When?'

'The night of the cleansing.'

'No.'

'What do you mean, no?'

'What else did he say?'

'It would hurt you if I said anything. He was the one help-ing me, not you. You don't know what you're doing.'

'I took the spirit out of you,' Kifli said.

'Yes, I know you did.'

'Not him.'

'I know.'

'I did it.'

'I believe you.'

The room was hazy, bloated, vulgar. Colourless. Arrogant, insufficient. Rocking, soothing her nausea, turning grey. Rusted out with the snap of a magician's fingers. A *bomoh*'s song and dance. What was Kifli to her anyway? She didn't know. She didn't have the language to put a name to him.

IT WAS NIGHT. RACHEL&KIFLI were buried in the illusion that they were alone. They simply forgot about the spirit when they were swimming in the river of love. Then, before they had a chance to catch their breath, Zulkanyan would remind them he was there: a streak of orange light, a screeching train in Kifli's ear. Every contradiction exists in totality. Every contradiction is possible when more than one soul inhabits a body.

Rachel was getting used to the idea that the old man and the boy came together. It wasn't as hard as one might think, going from one to the other, having every story repeated from another point of view.

She had tapped into an expanded universe, through an altered state. It hadn't come out of a guru's mouth in India or a yogi's hands in Nepal; it came in Singapura, the lion city; not in the mangrove swamps where the dog-faced water snake lived, but at Raffles, a five-star hotel, for her personal viewing pleasure. It came through a Malay Muslim, *Sejarah Melayu*, whose people have a preoccupation with arsenic and other poisons, cunningly administered to produce symptoms of lingering disease.

No one would believe her.

For one brief moment it occurred to Rachel that Kifli could be a fake. He could be making the whole thing up. How would she ever know? Except for the way she felt and her bouts of sleeping. Except for her dreams and the knowings that came into her. This could all be a play, it could be a display of lies and illness. Maybe this guy was sick in the head. Maybe she had a malaria fever and was in a bed at Raffles dreaming.

Zulkanyan must have had as much of a beard as an old Asian man can grow. He stroked it around the man-boy's hairless chin. Rachel imagined it pointed like the glass peaks of the Himalayas. He turned his head. 'My child,' he said, then, 'blah, blah, blah, blah.'

THE NIGHT OF RACHEL'S accursed cleansing Kifli had tried to leave. When he returned to his body he said, 'I need to see my mother.'

'I'm afraid, Kifli, please don't go.'

When he lay on the bed she pulled herself over his soft flesh.

'Tell me that you love me again and that you'll die without me,' she said. And then, 'Even though you've only known me a few days.'

They fell to sleep in the bed closest to the wall. The one with the picture landscape hanging over it. With birds in the sky.

She kicked him in her sleep. She woke up crazy, said, 'Stop bothering me.'

He said, 'I'm so cold. I'm sorry, I'm shaking.'

'What are you talking about? There's no way to tolerate this heat.' She threw off the covers. He reached down and pulled them back up.

Then, something he wasn't prepared for. She sat up like a board and stuck out her arm like a weather vane, her index finger straight as a ruler, aimed at him. Her eyes spat. She could have sent him through the wall if she had pointed to it.

She was full of power, big as the room. Each time she took a breath she grew larger. Kifli cowered like a little thing.

Foul and guarded she said, 'Get out, you're killing me.'

It was too late to run. He stood up straight, opening his chest so she would have a clear mark.

She could kill him if she wanted to.

Whatever witch she was.

He called her name.

'Rachel.'

There was wind.

'Rachel.'

His voice was small. A guilty little bad boy's voice.

'Rachel. It's me.'

'Who the fuck are you?'

'Kifli Talib.'

She dropped her head to her chest, her arm to her side. She looked up and smiled at his pathetic state. 'Don't cry. I'm so hot. Why did you turn the air off?'

'It's freezing.'

Now that he was afraid of her she wanted to prop him up and save him. She just wanted some cool air.

'Come back to bed. Don't cry, tell me about your monkey.'

He loved her like a child. He loved her as if she were a child, and with a child's love.

Getting back into bed with her was the moment of his surrender. He knew after that, she could make him her slave and he would take it. He was going to stay and be her love slave and she could kill him if she wanted to.

Whatever was going on was between his spirit and hers.

'Come on,' she said, nudging her nose into his neck. 'Tell me about your monkey.'

When I served in the army, I had a vision that an animal would be coming to me. During a day off, I was in Tumburo, a nearby jungle village. I spotted a native man carrying a baby monkey. It still had its eyes closed. He was going to eat her, so I bought her and carried her back to camp.

This monkey came to the world, opened her eyes and saw me, a human being. Oh, my father is a man, she thought.

I had to feed her with an eyedropper, milk, fruits chewed very fine. She didn't have to climb for food. She ate from a plate. She liked lychee better than apples, anything sweet with a bit of sugar, mints, chewing gum. She kept her neck bloated with nuts and lychee to spit up and eat later when she was alone.

We lived together, ate together, showered together. She felt good when she slept near my head. Before I got into bed I threw ants over myself, then she would be busy looking for them, like lice. It eased my mind when she played with my eyebrows and combed her fingers through my hair.

She was free. Everybody loved her, but whenever I called for her, she would leave any handsome soldier and come.

One day she brought a kitten to the barracks. She was pulling on my pants and pointing to her mouth to get food for the kitten. She wanted another friend. From that day, I had a kitten next to me in bed with the monkey wrapped around it. After a few months the cat started resisting, the monkey became afraid of her. Finally she agreed to let her go and be a cat.

She wanted to smoke cigarettes like me. Messed up the barracks trying to light matches. I needed her to fear fire, so I paid a friend twenty dollars to burn her fingers. I didn't have the heart to do it. She was a baby to me. After that she stayed away from matches so when I asked her to bring my cigarettes, she wouldn't bring the light.

When I finished the army I tried to bring her home. She arrived dead, with blood coming through her ears and nose. It must have been from the air pressure in the cargo hold. From that time I didn't want anything to do with another animal.

All that night Kifli lay awake shivering and thirsty and hungry. He could eat a cow and drink a river.

At a vanity mirror, a pink lipstick in her hand, melted to one side of its tube, strong like the black of her hair.

*Ring ring...Ring ring...* She picks up the phone.

'Hello.'

'My child,' says Zulkanyan, 'you must leave Singapore.' If this war was going to be won, Zulkanyan would have to separate the two lovers. Long enough to get Kifli back in line. To have the guru lecture him about the evil Jews, and for Zulkanyan to punish Kifli into submission.

How does she speak to a spirit over the phone? It is absurd to consider conversing across a wire with a spirit who lived before the invention of electricity. She hangs up and bursts out laughing. These kinds of scenes only happen in movies. How cool is that? Holy shit.

Everything was a test. How loyal would she be to the spirit against the Malay man-boy? How much would she believe? How much would she take?

If Zulkanyan had shown her the magic she longed to see she might have scared herself to death with it; at the very least she would have sucked back her soul that was seeping out of its membrane sac faster than he could grab hold of it. The spirit Zulkanyan was saccharine sweet to Rachel. The man-boy was resisting and it was better just to send Rachel home. As for Kifli, he wondered if he could go with her. Could she find him a job? Teach him to read English novels? Marry him?

She looked at Kifli's passport photo, a borrowed suit and wide cotton tie. He looked sinister in black and white.

When it was time to leave Singapore Rachel wasn't sure she was ready. She was a beggar who had received her wish. Until she returned to Singapore she'd have to memorize the images of Raffles Hotel's corridors. And Kifli's face.

Having no room for another one of his stories, no resistance to their dense and sultry content, she flung herself into a rattan chair. 'Kifli.' She grabbed his hand as he reached for the suitcase handle. She put the silk flower he had given her to her nose. It smelled like the basement of Lynton's house.

Kifli was about to say something, she could tell. His eyes went bright as he looked up at her and then he sighed, lowering his gaze to her feet. He did this three or four times and then, instead of speaking, he kissed her lips. Bit through their red-purple lining.

They thrashed against each other, their cheeks, pelvises, heads. Their legs. They turned on their sides and all their half-shut doors flew open and the contents of him crashed into the contents of her. Everything was open and swinging and banging and smashing.

Just before Rachel disappeared through the departures gate she joined her hands together as she had seen Buddhist monks do over candles in the foothills of Kathmandu. She hooked her thumbs under her chin, bent her head low, her waist slightly at the hinge. '*Namaste*,' she said to Kifli.

After Rachel's plane took off, Kifli sat on a bench in the airport writing her an old *Pantun*.

> *This waistcloth is of silk so gay*
> *That when you bathe you should not wet it.*
> *This game's for two of us to play;*
> *Should death result, do not regret it.*

DABBED WITH LEMON AND MANDARIN oils, she put on her leather flats and set out again into a world that made no sense, arriving in the scrum of an Aussie-rules football game. She imagined how light it would be in Sydney, Australia. The air less weighty, shadows shorter, narrower than in Singapore; she thought the English speakers inhabiting the Australian continent had confined their Gods to churches and fanatical enclaves like their British predecessors. The Aborigines, their Gods were in the heart of the land.

When Rachel stepped into the Sydney morning it was still black outside. The air danced in her throat as if a noose had been released from around her neck until she realized Singapore had followed her; it sat on top of her like the thing in the dark when she was a little girl feeling a shadow.

Another hotel. Coffee maker in the bathroom. Another phone beside a bed. Another two hours before the sun would appear. It was a dangerous time on the border of sunrise. The world was treacherous until the birds sang. Fear kept her from sleeping. The box of pain over her chest was back.

'They haven't gone, Kifli,'

'You're okay, Rachel. They're with me now.'

'Don't lie to me. They're in this room. Is Zulkanyan there?'

'I haven't heard from him since you left.'

'You have to come here. I need you.'

'I am there. Can't you feel me?'

She pulled the phone cord. 'Are you coming, yes or no?'

'I don't have any money.'

'I'll pay for the ticket. Don't hang up.'

Since she was a child she had searched hotel drawers for Bibles. Bibles in hotel rooms gave her the creeps, consulted as a last resort after desperate phone calls or when everything else in the room was overturned, but Rachel often looked to see what condition they were in. When they were untouched she cracked them open to the spine zipping through a flurry of pages just to hear new paper break the air. Transparent as an ocean wave were Bible pages.

Rachel yanked on the handle of the dresser between the two double beds. The cover of the Gideon lodged itself into the recesses of the drawer. She pushed her hand in and tucked the cover down so she could pull out. She placed it on the night table, the gold cross facing up.

On the phone to a synagogue Rachel said what her father had prepared her to say all her life—that she was a stranger who wanted a house of worship on Yom Kippur, the holiest of holy days, the Day of Atonement. She needed a roof under which to negotiate the future of the coming year with her ancestral God. By the laws of Sarah, Rebecca, Rachel and Leah, Abraham, Isaac and Jacob, they had to let her in. Rachel told Sam Rosenberg, the shul president, her name and country, that she belonged to the tribe.

He said yes, of course. He would have to inform security that she was coming. Two weeks earlier a bomb had exploded in a Jewish daycare in Melbourne.

In the summer of 1985 bombs were everywhere: Amritsar, Cyprus, Tel Aviv, Eritrea, Belfast, Beirut, washing up on the beach, hidden under buildings. When the bomb? Where the bomb? How big the bomb? Who did the bomb, so we can send one back?

1. Munich
2. Entebbe
3. Katyusha rockets to Kiriat Shmona
4. The green line in Lebanon

Buses, cars, hitchhikers, aeroplanes, lunch bags, garbage bins, phone booths. Rachel had an explosive in her head, tick, tick. Mortal time. She carried it with her to convene with God.

When Rachel entered the sanctuary, all the Kaddish lights on the memorial boards were lit to remember the dead. She saw an old woman who reminded her of Nana near the front of the upper balcony, which leaned over the men's parade, where the Torah lived behind a dark blue velvet curtain. The old woman was also early, maybe because she moved slowly and needed time to mount the stairs to the women's balcony, or maybe because she wanted time alone with her God.

She prayed. Prayers are like childhood smells, they bring back the past. ברוך אתה יי '*Baruch atah adonai*,' back to when she held her eyes shut under her hands while lighting the Sabbath candles, אלהינו מלך העולם '*Eloheynu melech ha-olam*.' The flame had flickered under the breath of her prayer, lurched up, tracking her as she turned her face from the heat. Her severed braid fell, the flame ran along her head. Under the prayer shawl her father had thrown over her singed scalp, she had known at once she was bald.

Hair was kindling wood.

Her father held her face the way we hold delicate objects of value. He tilted her head, running her tears into her ears, and instead of hearing her father's voice, she heard the inner workings of her body, a cold blowing powder. 'It's gone, Papa, my hair.'

She wouldn't let her father take the braid away from her. She slept with it under her pillow for a week. After that Papa made her bury it. Everything had to be put into the ground for when the Messiah came. 'What do you think will grow there, Papa?' He said that her hair was only a woman's vanity, but a few days later an apple seed rolled out of his hand and he planted it above her burned braid.

Now an old woman, Monya looked elegant, a fine grey felt hat, lids of rippling skin with ocean waves of blue powder spread thickly over them. She saw Rachel coming and quickly slid to the aisle, waving Rachel down with both hands. 'Just a minute, I've never seen you before.' She had rings of soft skin around her wrists.

'I'm a visitor,' Rachel said.

'Who do you belong to?'

'No one.'

'How did you get in?'

'I called,' Rachel said smiling at Monya—warm, like Nana's apple strudel and sticky bones. Monya's eyes darted around the upper sanctuary, but there was no one else there.

'Are you a terrorist?'

'No. I'm a tourist.'

'Are you an Arab? Are you a terrorist?'

'No.'

Rachel thought the cries coming out of Monya looked like falling books. 'It's okay,' she said, 'I'm a Canadian. I'm Jewish.'

Rachel opened her purse to show Monya there was nothing in it, like she had done at the border of the Sinai on her way to Egypt, where there wasn't a metal detector.

'See, Mr. Rosenberg said I could come.'

'You look like an Arab,' Monya said, wiping her cloudy eyes, spreading blue dust down her cheek.

'It's my French blood,' said Rachel.

Monya said, 'Don't forget what they did. It will happen again.'

'I know,' said Rachel, 'but I want to forget so I can carry on. So I can love.'

'That's because it didn't happen in your family.'

'Yes, it did, to all of us. I have a hiding place.'

Monya smiled. She said, 'There's light coming from your feet.'

THE CANTOR, THE MAN with the lovely voice and the hat with a roof, sang better and brighter than the mumbling, chanting men. At that moment Rachel thought of men as songs, songs that lift like Catherine's prayer, covering her with sacred text, begging at times in God's direction. Is it men, Rachel wondered, who have created my paganhood? With no altar in the synagogue for her to articulate. Banished from the Torah, from touching it, from being called to it for an *aliyah*. She wanted a prayer shawl too, to cover herself like a ghost with fringe. The rabbi led, but his direction was ambiguous to her. What? The oozing of light, women gossiping. When can we eat? How much longer? Did you know Barbara and Robert are getting a divorce? Rachel's father picking from the cherry tree in their backyard while her mother pinned a mauve hat over her head. A beautiful mauve hat that smelled like stale fasting breath. Her father's breath was cherry. The real prayers were kept private. And for first thing in the morning trying to push the dread away. Or for shivas. For the dead.

Rachel told God she was coming for deliverance on the Day of Atonement. And so pray the Cohanim: *Master of the world, I am yours, and my dreams are yours. I dreamed a dream and I know not what it means. May it be your will that all my dreams contain knowledge. If they require healing, heal them. As you turned the curse of evil to a blessing, so may you turn my dreams to good. Guard me, grace me and accept me. May you protect me because I have taken refuge in you.*

The sound she heard—the crank in her head—was the cinch of her body cooling.

She had unglued herself from almost everyone at home; they snapped back to their lives, their jobs and fashion, the vacations they took, the books they read and the charity they kept in their hearts. She did, however, have her trick of incorporating genetic maps into her body for the ones she wanted to keep. Amen.

*Dear God,*
*What the hell is going on?*
*Rachel*
*P.S. Just kidding, Nana.*

'Hello.'
'I miss you.
'I miss you too, *Sayang*. Happy New Year.'
'How did you know?'
'I heard it on the radio.'
'Oh.'

A scattered account to a taxi driver of her movements from Canada to Australia, 'When I met my family in Rome, the entire city was under restoration. Scaffolds surrounded buildings draped with white linen, as if the city was hiding or getting married. This, of course, was in August when the whole country is on holiday in the south. In India it's the women who are wrapped like monuments. They have such intoxicating midriffs that I had to keep reminding myself that many of them were starving.'

The rabbi was young and American with a slew of children in the kitchen running around his wife. He sat behind an enormous desk. He was half bald without having grown a compensating beard. On the top of his head was a knitted kippah insinuating modern thinking.

'The Torah forbids you to speak to spirits,' he said.

'Well, I didn't know that. I asked to speak to a Jewish dead person and no one came, so I spoke to a Muslim.'

'Did you sleep with him?'

'I'm not going to answer that.'

'They use sex to manipulate women.'

'Rabbi, who doesn't?'

'You're damaging your soul and you're making jokes?'

'I'm trying to find out...'

'Stop talking to them.'

'That's it?'

'It's a sin.'

'Phh.'

'Your sleeping is depression.'

'Rabbi, who do you think built the pyramids?'

'Do you know how many children I've seen corrupted by gurus and religious pranksters?'

The rabbi rose and placed his hands over the glass-framed photo of the Lubavitch Rebbe. He took a deep breath. 'Did he give you drugs?'

Rachel plugged straight into the rabbi's eyes.

'You don't believe me, do you? They don't treat me like a mindless idiot.'

'Wait, wait,' he said. 'I'm listening. Please.'

'You've put these rules in front of me since I was a kid and the first time I rely on them they drop out from under me. I find out they're make-believe.'

'Rules are for order,' said the rabbi. 'Everyone has to be included. But there are laws, hidden mystical forces in you and the universe. What do you need?'

'I'm not crazy.'

'Haven't you been listening? You think I work with cults because I don't believe? Thought has great power. It's God's competition. I believe you, but I can't compete with magical illusion or altered states of consciousness.'

'I'm not asking you to.'

'Yes, you are.'

He looked flabby white. Rachel was sure he had breakfast stains somewhere on his shirt. She liked him, and wanted to tell him to go fuck himself. Interpreting her experience as if he knew what it was. He was probably jealous, she thought.

'Maybe God's saving me,' she said. 'Comes in many disguises, right?'

'Rachel, we have good Jewish men here. I don't say that without affection. Fall in love, get married, have a family. You're a Jewish soul.'

'My mother converted.'

'All the better.'

'Not even orthodox, to you I'm not a Jew.'

'You have a sign on your forehead that says "Jewish soul," see it?'

He pointed to the glass reflection of his desk. 'Look at yourself.'

She leaned over the glass and looked at a photo tucked under the desktop of the rabbi's daughter dressed as Queen Esther at a Purim party.

'The great rabbi, the Baal Shem Tov, ended up flat on his back in his garden playing with mystical incantations. He'd fallen four storeys, could have killed himself, and he couldn't remember what had happened. Who needs it? Life is hard enough the way it is.'

'No offence,' she said, 'but you don't get it.'

'Really?'

The rabbi closed his office door.

'You think Jews don't know about magic? *Abrah kadabra*, you think that's Greek? One story, that's all I'm giving you. I know a doctor...'

*Nana,*

*Don't get angry, but my story was better than the rabbi's. He really tried though. He spread open his arms and flapped them like wings.*

*It's hard when you're only repeating someone else's experience.*
*Love Me*

*Lennart,*
*This is a kangaroo. Looks a bit like you. Ha ha ha.*
*P.S. Kifli's coming.*

And so it was that Kifli was accused of stealing stamps from the drawer at the Raffles Hotel registration desk. He said he had lent the key to another porter but that didn't matter because it was Kifli's responsibility anyway. He was dismissed in the morning and could have taken a bus to the travel agency and then home but he walked. He needed the calm and monotonous pit-a-pat of his shoes along the sidewalk while he figured things out in his head. I'm a good man, he thought. I don't throw litter on the ground. I give up my seat on the metro to old women. Kifli neatly folded some clothes into a vinyl brown suitcase: jeans and brown polyester pants, blue cotton shorts, seven pairs of underwear, a faded Raffles shirt with the recipe for a Singapore sling printed on the back, runners, a black sweater, and a few T-shirts along with his sunglasses and couple of pens in his shirt pocket and his wallet in the back pocket of his pants. His passport in his hand. And then on his way out the door his mother told him never to come back. All Kifli wanted was to get back to the arms he loved. It had been an eternity since his lips had kissed the top of her head as she slept.

THE NEON SIGN OUTSIDE their window buzzed a pink shadow across the room. One of the letters was almost dead. The *H* occasionally would stutter and half of it would glow:
'ASTORIA OTEL'

Kifli went repeatedly to the window—flashes of white skin under short skirts, leaning into cars. There were English voices in the street. Giggling night women from the Southern Cross district. Car doors opened then slammed shut. Rachel&Kifli kept the same hours as the prostitutes. In a way they lived in the same blue-blackening. A double life, defined by the rise and tumble of the sun.

The sheets were thin, part cotton, part synthetic. There was no Bible in the night table drawer. The room was already a mess. Every time Rachel went to the bathroom, she tripped over her shoes.

The phone never rang and they didn't call out.

With the door shut, three flights up and a twist around the banister, Rachel felt trapped. It was hot. She kicked off the covers.

'If Zulkanyan can't tell me who built the pyramids, Kifli, what good is he?'

Kifli turned from the window.

'I don't know.'

'Do you think he knows everything?'

'I don't know, Rachel.'

The Astoria Hotel was a good place for the spirit Zulkanyan to begin unravelling his plan without earthly interventions. He had directed them to a hotel where most guests didn't stay all night. By three in the morning Kifli&Rachel were the only ones left. It was dark even with the lights on. Two weak bulbs under a plate of glass painted with swivels of gold, the kind of light that casts more shadows than illuminations. What light there was only brought confusion into the room. There was a fan, just as always, stirring the dim, murky air.

Kifli moved through shades of grey and blue-grey to get to the switch. He closed the lights with his fingertips. Just before the light cut out, Rachel memorized the triangle of muscle at his abdomen, the first thing she reached for when he climbed into bed. He reached for the wall.

He settled over Rachel the way he had seen a woman outside pose for a john, one arm behind his head, neon stripes blinking across his back. 'I'm losing you,' he said.

She said, 'Do you know what I am, *Sayang*? I'm a jellyfish spread thin across the ocean. So thin, you can't even see me, can you?' She closed her eyes. He sang her a Malay love song. 'Make your voice sweet,' said Zulkanyan. 'Suckle her life away.' Rachel loved the feeling without knowing what it was.

She missed him when he was sleeping, she ached. She felt down to see if he was hard, swept her legs around his waist so he wore her like a sash. She did it while Kifli was unconscious. As soon as she kissed his lips he moaned river dreams.

He tried to push her off. She said, 'Let's do it again.' He couldn't speak. He was saying a prayer in his head, so it was his eyes, bolt cold, that said no. 'No, no.' He slid out of her with the turn of his hip. The prop flew out of the window. The window came down, *thunk*, in her head. Barely conscious, her black lips spoke from this world and the other side. Kifli sat up like a board and squeezed his hands around her neck. He strangled her until she smiled. And then he let her go. He loves her so much he could have snapped her neck, filled her with arsenic, eaten her up.

She isn't afraid. Who is he but her other half? Wherever she's going, he is too. Whatever he does, whatever—his tiny bleeding bites on her arms feel like antiseptic. She mistakes his hands for love, and his gesture for passion. 'Get out of here, Rachel, I'm no good.'

After sitting on the window ledge for an hour listening to the high-pitched voices, watching the prostitutes come and go, he went back to her and crawled inside. 'An hour's bus ride from my house in the early morning and I'm covered in blood. Some ears in my pocket.'

'How many?' she said.

He wanted to be accurate so he motioned as if to pile the ears in his hand as he counted them out for her. Then he said, 'A human doesn't have to take responsibility for a spirit.' Kifli is expanding and diminishing at the same time. Increasing as a man—shrinking as conductor.

'Not all of them were killed right away,' he said.

During the mornings they were like any young couple forging a relationship. They had to eat, they had to make plans about what they wanted to do during the day. Rachel read the shop window: *$4.00 a lb. $1.50 to fold*. There weren't enough whites to do a full load so that would be extra. Kifli carried the laundry inside Rachel's violet sari.

'How much money do you have, Kifli?'

'Fifty Singapore dollars. Do you want me to change it at the bank?'

'In India fifty dollars would feed a village.'

'I'm costing you too much.'

'Don't be silly. Do you think I would pay to launder my clothes and leave you to wash yours in the sink? Have them hanging all over the room?'

She had taken a pocketful of Nana's bank notes on her search for meaning. She had planned from the beginning to stash away enough cash for a plane ticket home from wherever—whenever. Who knows, she might have to buy herself out of slavery, or possibly meet a prince and need a beaded gown, it might become imperative for her to have American dollars for a hospital bill, or for a payoff to get to a secret cave or out of a tour in the jungle with an envious guide. She was just watching her back.

Now it was money to bring Kifli back to her—money for hotels and restaurants, taxi fares, tanning lotions and ice cream, laundry. She said she would be spending the same for hotels and taxis if she was alone. When bills came Kifli looked out the window, or he went to the men's room, or bent down to retrieve a napkin he had dropped from his knees to the floor. This time he stood in the corner of the laundromat smoking a Camel.

When Kifli handed the sari to Rachel everything fell onto the ground: sweaty T-shirts, jeans, flaking crotches, the Fiorucci dress she wore in the graveyard, the night shirt she had worn in Nepal, cotton shorts, stained with both Rachel and Kifli's skin cells and salts, hair and whatever it was that escaped from Kifli when Zulkanyan came.

'I'm sorry, Rachel.'

'It's too damn early to be smoking, Kifli.'

'Sorry.'

Rachel saw a pair of bronze Buddha bookends through the window of an antique store. The dealer smiled, she'd been around. She took hold of one of the amulets around her neck and mumbled something under her breath. On a crowded table amongst sugar shakers, silver pickle forks, ivory beads and a tortoiseshell hair comb, a silver monkey wearing a fez sat smiling. Rachel picked it up and checked under its feet for the price, the same way she would have done with a pair of shoes. When she looked up, the antique dealer was squinting into Kifli's paraffin face. Her Fu dog leapt up and charged at Kifli, snarling and bugging its eyes out. 'She never barks like this,' said the dealer.

Rachel resumed looking for the price tag, searching now on the monkey's back.

'There's a reason why you're attracted to that candlestick,' the dealer said.

'I guess so.'

'Oh, I'd say so. Objects talk.'

'Yes, I know.' Rachel had her own relationships to objects, especially tarot cards and Ouija boards. She was drawn to lockets and pocket watches, vulnerable to the influence of ivories and energies of previous owners, whose fears made their possessions cold.

The dog's little fangs had latched onto Kifli's pant leg.

Kifli stood still as stone.

'Sushi, sweetie, get off of him. Go to your bed.'

Reluctantly, the dog released the Malay man-boy.

'I'm so sorry. She's never bitten anyone. Of course, we don't know who you are.'

'I'm from Canada,' Rachel said.

'And him?'

'He's with me.'

'Well, you see, we don't know anything about you two.'

'No, you don't.'

'I like your bracelets.'

'Thank you, me too.'

'From where?'

'Everywhere.'

'And him?'
'He's with me.'


*Dear Lennart,*
*We only exist when others observe us.*
*We only become people through the eyes of another.*


She was bouncing on the bed doing jumping jacks, her toes pointed. 'Why don't you let me breathe? I want to think, can't think with you clutching my brain.' Rachel's heart raced like a siren. The box of pain over her heart was constricting. Her veins seemed crowded. Outside, in the scorching heat, insects vaporized.

Kifli slammed the door on his way out. He had never slammed the door before. She kept touching the ceiling, harder each time, as if the roof might give way. It wasn't as spacious as she thought it would be without him there.

He didn't have a key and he was worried she might not let him back in. He was trying to stay away from her because he didn't know what he was capable of, with Zulkanyan screaming in his ear. He took the stairs, tentatively knocked. 'Who is it?' 'Me.' 'Who?' He didn't answer. As soon as she opened the door he said, 'Do you make love with Zulkanyan?'

'What?'

'Do you love him?'

She pulled Kifli into the room. 'Don't disappear like tha
I thought you weren't coming back.'

'I'm not your servant, Rachel.'

'Oh my God.'

'What?'

'Do you lose time when we make love?'

'No.'

'Are you sure?'

'I don't know what you do with him, Rachel.'

'Kifli, he's an old man. Look at what he's told you abo
sex and he's probably never done it.'

Outside the confines of hotel rooms their world became va
Kifli&Rachel found their way to the structured, clean defir
tion of the Sydney art gallery: strong amber walls, paintin
hanging by nails and wire, designated culture, creatir
beliefs—ways of looking, evolving, the way people might ha
if they had left themselves alone to frolic in their psych
mumble. And in Rachel's mind the moment she stepp
across the threshold of the Sydney art gallery: the totem p
in the Royal Ontario Museum and depictions of hell and pu
gatory she had seen on the enormous canvases of Europ
Leonardo's water machines, Rousseau, the Tower of Londo
Anne Boylen's head, fleurs-de-lis, Peter Max, Faust and fi
Lynton's hands, Kifli's water.

They are always asking each other to see things.

She pointed to the first haystack hanging on the wall in a room full of haystacks and said, 'Monet. What do you think?'

'What am I supposed to see?' he said.

'Anything.'

'I don't know,' he said.

'It's not a test,' she said.

Rachel looked at each haystack in the room, faster and faster from one to the other like a whirling dervish, violent blue becoming bright yellow, then pink of all kinds. *See in the rain—the cold night coming.*

Faster than the painter Monet could capture his chameleon mounds, Kifli could turn into Zulkanyan. This is how she loves Kifli. When she circles him he is a matrix.

*Look at this haystack*
*Look at it again*
*Night—another life*
*A different eye*

Rachel thought she would be as brilliant as a Monet on the wall if she had clarity. She would be as beautiful as she was when Lynton loved her.

*Forgive me, Monet, I am blind.*
*This darkness often feels like it might be the light.*
*Come to tea and be my lover. Empty my pail of sorrow.*

Rachel laughed out loud. Not from her throat, where she usually just forced a smile forward into sound, she laughed like a Buddha. From her belly. Ha ha ha. Hee hee hee. Hoo hoo hoo. After that she fell into a state of excruciating anxiety. *Oh God, Dana fucked my angel. Do you know what it's like to open your mouth and push the air and it won't make a sound? There's a wall in the dip of my throat where everything stops.*

*Why did I want to kill myself? Why not them? And no*
*while I am here under your light I will tell you that I loved hi.*
*even after Dana. I still took him into my bed.*

Rachel saw Kifli from a gallery window walking aimless.
through the grounds, talking to himself. *Look at the poor bo*
*He makes me sick, unable to have a single thought of his own.*

He was becoming suffocating; he would never fit into h
world. And why, she thought, if there was only one world d
so few things fit together? For example, she knew Kifl
mother would never invite her over for dinner—and wors
she might never want to go.

She liked spying on him. He never left her alone. If sl
hadn't seen him from the window she would have thougl
he'd disappeared again. It was so unfair that she had to tal
care of him all the time. She never knew when she wou
need to sleep and here he was going out of his mind in t
middle of the day without even warning her.

What a weak foolish boy he was.

The man-boy down there was her food.

She hated him sometimes.

In the garden sanctuary below, Rachel tapped him on t
shoulder. He sneered. She said, 'Where the hell is Kifli?'

He walked passed her. She jumped in front of him. I
pushed her to the ground, then climbed on a bridge raili
and looked down to the road, the way people do in the movi
when they're going to jump.

'Shit,' she said, grabbing the back of his shirt and pulling him to the grass. 'Shit, shit, shit.' Rachel backed away. She sat down under a tree and said every Hebrew word she could think of, 'שמע ישראל יי אלהינו יי אחד, *Shemah yisrael adonai eloheynu adonai echad. Hear O Israel, the Lord our God, the Lord is one.* דלת קטנה, אני רחל, אור ההשראה, *Delet ketanah, anee Rachel, ore ha-hashra-ah. Small door, I am Rachel, light of inspiration.*'

Zulkanyan came over to her, laughing. Rachel began to sob.

'What's so funny?'

'You're praying. Good.'

'Can't you straighten him out? I can't stand it any longer.'

'Our boy is confused,' said Zulkanyan.




'Where were you?' Kifli said. 'Are you all right?'

'Stop asking me that. If I was all right I wouldn't be crying, would I?'

Kifli looked at her as if she were all he had.

'It's hard to protect you, Rachel.'

'Oh stop it. You're just making me crazy.'

'Is that what he told you?'

'Am I, Kifli? Am I crazy?'

'I don't think so.'

'You don't think so?'

'No, okay, you're not crazy.'

'If you asked me, Kifli, I'd say you were crazy.'

'Some day you will be my wife. We will make peace between the Muslims and the Jews.'

'You see what I mean?'

'That's not crazy, Rachel.'

Rachel's dream.

*Lynton wanted to show Rachel something in the bushes. Excited, he took her hand and told her to follow him. They reached a construction site where Lynton pointed up a hill to huge blocks of hash situated as the stones in Egypt that blocked the entrance to the pyramids.*

*Rachel became frantic. A fire started and they ran away. Then men were carrying away Lynton and they wouldn't let Rachel see him. He was screaming for her but she couldn't get to him. Many days later he was carried back, wrapped in blankets and seeming very small. Not in good health.*

*Rachel knelt beside the bed and pulled the blankets away. Lynton was very thin and she couldn't find his legs.*

How easy, as a subtle ride of wind, the spirit Zulkanyan entered Kifli—so light a breeze it would barely tilt a Garnet Pitta's wing. The words from his mouth a rolling grassy field that smelled to Rachel like the air on the last day of school. In front of the mirror in their bedroom he pushed her bracelets over her limp hands. 'Careful,' she said, 'my nails are still wet.' He had just painted them slushy pink.

Kifli's thumbs and index fingers formed a tent, and then they emerged one by one.

Bowing to Rachel while her slushy-pink polish dried.

'The grandmother of the Silat martial art thanks you.'

Bowing.

'The grandfather of the Silat martial art thanks you.'

Bowing.

'The mother of the Silat martial art thanks you.'

Again bowing.

'The father of the Silat martial art thanks you for letting us perform a cleansing.'

Rachel bowed to each of them, didn't utter a word.

*Knock, knock.*

Who's there?

The threat is in the brain.

The threat is in sleep.

The threat is in the room.

Rachel was a slovenly dreamer.

*A crowd of angry women in beautiful silk saris stood around her with rocks in their hands, jeering and ready to stone her to death. She raised her arms to protect her face. Then, even before the first stone was cast, Kifli's mother sailed across the sky, showering Rachel with flecks of gold, which fell to the ground like snow crystals and appeased the crowd.*

THE WHOLE TOWN OF PORT DOUGLAS WAS: a pie shop, the Central Bar, a grocery store, a fancy restaurant and a sacred seven-mile stretch of velvet sand and happy birds along a tree-lined shore that led into miles of sugar cane. Port Douglas was a secluded town, small and hushed. The sea and the blowing trees were the loudest gossipers, but not the only ones—the local people slid their tongues around the young woman who walked down the main thoroughfare leaning into the Malay man-boy who shimmied up coconut trees picking ripe. The dreams of Port Douglas still quivered in the early air. Once anchored at its sight, the *Beagle*, and the *Will-o'-the-Wisp*. Captain James Cook on ship's time, noon to noon, unlike the civilians, midnight to midnight. Or the Aborigine's dreamtime. Rachel&Kifli, slowtime. All connected to the golden chain.

He was gentler than sleep. Over their bed the ceiling fan was swirling in the morning of the coming rains. The humidity rose from their bodies. She lay over Kifli as he held her in the heat. His long bones and pockmarks spread out on the bed, his skin watery like the fluid of glass. She saw the reflection of her eyelashes blinking in the irises of his eyes. They waited, like that, in their private room under the pressure of the monsoon until the temperature was unbearable. Rachel looking at him like the porcelain doll stares out the window of the Chinese toy store on Orchard Road. She knew that when Kifli's eyelids shuddered, he was ready to merge. They left their bodies and swam.

Together they have natural and superstitious ways. A man-boy and a sensitive who have minimal attachment to the physical world. They are seekers who are mesmerized by each other while looking for themselves.

They could be an illusion.

In the sky over the green jungle by the back door there was always a flash of brilliance before the rains came. Her body in the sun.

Kifli asked if she believed in falling in love, immediately, the first moment—before language. It amused her that he spoke of love when a deep spell had been cast on her, causing her heart to constrict. She told him she thought she was dying.

Commuting between the two worlds would soon drain her. Passing from here to the other side—parallel equations that must steal from each other for resolve. She wanted both. Everyone does at the beginning. The glorious sleep of death, and the radiant awakening.

Kifli loved Rachel no matter where she was, pale and exquisite, or breathless. The closer she drew to Zulkanyan, the less she cared about anything else. When she was fresh with life she was animated and frothy; otherwise, her box of pain stabbed at her, making it difficult to breathe. Kifli and Zulkanyan took her back and forth between two worlds. Eventually she'd be able to do it herself. Kifli realizes Rachel is losing her fear of death. He wants to break his contract with Zulkanyan and give up his powers to try and save her; as an un-possessed man he might contain the dense human material needed to call her back.

Instead of putting a cold cloth across her head to revive her, Kifli flung Rachel's books onto her bed and begged her to read. He also wanted to hear her stories, about Nana's car stalling on the railway tracks when a train was coming, what Lynton's letter to Dana said when they were lovers, how Byron limped across a dance floor.

Rachel asked him to tell her his recipes for a variety of gorengs, about his circumcision when he was fifteen, what he was wearing, how long it took him to recover. How long he cried. Longer than a baby eight days old? His telling brought her comfort for the transitions. Smoking tobacco, drinking coffee. Death, the absence of abandonment—maybe something she could trust.

'You don't have to kill me to own my soul,' she said. 'You could never take me with force.'

'Rachel, I won't always be able to help you,' he said.

'So do it now, while you still can.' Those were her words but her hair stood on end, a cold wind flew into Kifli's face.

She watched the palm fluttering over them. Kifli was prone to going into trance in the morning just after they stirred beneath the heat. It was a long time ago, but Rachel remembered the fear that began before she ever reached Singapore; she used to taste it every morning, even attempted to cry it out loud—since she was thirteen, a phlegm in her throat that she couldn't swallow. During those times she hated frail things. She wanted to break them and get it over with.

The first time Rachel noticed the spirit masquerading as the man-boy, he was brushing her hair at the beach. In broad daylight, in front of the whole world he was brushing her hair, and she knew because the nuance of his movement and the density of his body suddenly, slightly, changed.

'Is that you, Zulkanyan?'

'How did you know?'

The light fetched brocades of red that the sun had glistened in her black hair. Next to Kifli&Rachel on the beach, two girls at either end of a skipping rope, turning, and the third jumps in:

*Cinderella dressed in yella*
*Went upstairs to kiss her fella,*
*By mistake, she kissed a snake;*
*How many doctors did it take?*
*One, two, three, four...*

A letter from Lennart had been forwarded from the American Express office in Sydney.

> *Dear Rachel,*
> *Wearing a sari doesn't make you an Indian. I feel guilty for coming home too early.*
> *Love,*
> *Lennart*

Rachel has come in from the beach. Kifli looks up from one of her books. 'What's the water like?' Because in Port Douglas, it's the reef and shallows that are dangerous, like the Nile or Lake Dahl—this time, invisible jellyfish.

'I don't know,' Rachel said. 'I didn't touch it.'

Kifli was in their room moaning like a river, thinking Rachel shared herself with Zulkanyan every time Kifli lost time. Maybe when he returned to her hunger it was only to consummate what the girl and the spirit hadn't figured out how to do yet. Kifli wanted his own life. He wanted his own life so he could relinquish it to Rachel. Kifli's arms twitched, his legs jerked. His headaches felt like they were blowing his head off. Rachel elbowed his side. 'Wake up. It's the middle of the day.' He remained unmoved so Rachel got out of bed. Kifli continued to shudder. 'Someone talk to me,' Rachel said.

'He's busy. What do you want?' said Zulkanyan. He looked around the way a spirit does, tilting his head to his shoulder as if his ears were his eyes, his eyes half closed. Rachel picked Kifli's shirt off the floor and pulled it over her head.

Her voice rattled.

'Where's Kifli?'

'He's down there.'

'He is? Where?'

'Having a good dream.'

'Is he?'

'He's all right.'

'He's been strange.'

'He only wants to be a man.'

'Why?'

'You.'

'Me?'

'Yes.'

'Why?'

'Love.'

'Shit.'

'Yes.'

'When's he coming back?'

'In the morning.'

'Come on, you're not serious. What am I supposed to do all night? What will he do if he gives you up? He's never been alone.'

'He'll have you.'

'I can't be there all the time, you have to do it.'

'He doesn't want me anymore.'

That evening when Kifli woke up she said, 'You've known Zulkanyan your whole life.' He said, 'I know what I'm doing.' She said, 'Bullshit.' He said, 'Fuck, Rachel, you don't understand.' She said, 'Fine.'

'Where are you going?' he said.

'To take a bath.'

'Can I come?'

'No.'

She was heading for the bedroom to get some clothes when she turned around and marched back. 'I got my period today, Kifli, so I'm unclean. You better stay away from me.'

'I don't believe that anymore,' he said.

'No? Why? You believed it a few weeks ago. Did I change your mind? Just tell me one original thought that has ever come into your head. You think you can give up Zulkanyan and think everything I tell you now?'

'No.'

'So?'

'I'm sorry.'

'For what?'

'You're angry.'

'Yeah, but you don't even know why.'

Kifli stared at her in disbelief. 'No one told me to love the enemy, Rachel. Maybe that was stupid too.'

She unbuttoned his shirt she was wearing and dropped it

next to the bed. 'I was so bored. Do you know you've been out all afternoon?'

Rachel kissed him. She licked around the rim of his nose. She turned to face him, then bent her knee so her foot could rub against soft skin. 'Umm,' she said. Blindly she traversed his chest, opening his heart to her as if the flesh wasn't there. Within each other's magnetic pull, nothing could keep them apart.

This time he turned her over. He watched his hand between her thighs. He came faster than usual and cried right away.

'Shh,' she said.

He wiped off her back with his shirt. Then he said, '*Sayang?*'

'Yeah?'

'When people die with hatred they still want to hurt people.'

'What are you talking about?'

'You believe everything I say to you too, Rachel. Do you think a holy man would ask me to kill?'

Rachel stares at Kifli in disbelief.

'You think he's so nice to you? He's taking care of you by blowing on your silver bangle and turning it white. He was sucking your life out of it. You slept for two days after that. I've been protecting you.' He lowers his voice. 'Zulkanyan is not the priest. He pretends. He hates everyone. I don't know what kind of witch you are or why he's so interested in you, but he hates you too. I am the one who takes care of you.'

Her fear tastes like the metal of blood.

'I don't know, Kifli.' She stormed into the bathroom and slammed the flimsy plywood door. Kifli heard the lock. She emerged an hour later. 'Are you coming?'

He jumped up from the bed.

After all his warnings, Rachel was more intrigued by the Malay man-boy's collaborations than afraid of her own death. He was a deep-sea creature who kept Rachel alive by acquiescing to Zulkanyan, slowly guiding her to her demise. At the age of twenty-four she felt she was still immortal, and contained the books she had read from a classical education.

Kifli's stories satisfied Rachel's ideas of beauty and framed them with suggestions of morbid deeds. Murderous words stuffed down into his stomach filled with white rice, puffy and soaking in bile, his hands calmly in his lap, Rachel entranced in front of him like he was a television set. Up close thousands of black lines made up the picture like the slits of a python's eyes.

Kifli would rather be deaf than listen to the foul grinding of hate in his ear. He had his own appetite—his own discovery of her. He could impress her himself. After all, it was he who was called by the guru to bring help from the spirit world. Even if Zulkanyan knew what Rachel was thinking, Kifli didn't want to know from him. Zulkanyan lied. He was generous with ambiguities, making the best of what the man-boy had to offer, physical conditioning and flexibility, a willingness to kill.

Kifli wanted to be the only one peering out of his own eyes. He was suffocating in the bones he had the right to claim. This was his world and his time to be in it. When

Kifli&Rachel collided they held each other still, and that made Kifli feel whole, until Zulkanyan interfered. 'She treats you like you're her monkey.'

Zulkanyan tried to sneak up on her, a deep slow breath, the way Rachel breathed through a regulator when she was diving in the Red Sea. He became a ventilation mask.

She trembled. She didn't know what he was capable of so she venerated him. Before speaking, Zulkanyan wanted to soothe her awe. 'My child,' he stroked her forehead.

'I must go,' he told her almost as soon as he arrived. 'I only came to tell you to believe in God. Take care of Kifli. He loves you.'

Kifli drifted back, took in Rachel's face and began to pray. How much time had he lost? What did he say? Did he do anything to push her away? Had he been punished?

Zulkanyan's visitations reminded Rachel of when she swam alone in Lake Erie at dusk, entering the water just as the insects came hovering and night things opened their eyes. Rachel imagined that in the blue of her immersion there were big monsters that ate people, huge creatures with the blistering skin of a rusting hull. At night the world transformed behind an inky curtain.

As the sun set below the horizon, Rachel became agitated. The fading light reminded her of how much she couldn't get done before she died, what she wouldn't see or understand, whom she would never meet. At night, shadows of her indelible past...

No one ever wanted to talk about what went on in the darkness of solitude.

Passion is fed by the cooling veins of night.

In a postcard to Nana she described the night as a woman's feet with patches of dark green almost black between her toes.

Burning houses are more vivid in the dark and Rachel was a burning house. And in her dreams: *The cloth the Tibetan yogi had placed over her in Nepal was removed; over her naked body stood surgeons and machinery, under her back was the slab of an operating theatre. She was not fully anaesthetized and there was trouble in her body. They brought in a woman to sew the final stitches. Rachel's mother.*

She wakes up. 'Let's go to the beach. It's a full moon. The animals will all come out.' He pulls on his pants. She says, 'Don't you have a pair of jeans?' He says, 'Yes.' And when he puts them on she says, 'Don't you have a pair without the pockets in the front so they stop staring at us on the street?' He says, 'No. I don't think it's my pockets, do you?' Kifli's rubbing paperbark leaves against his forehead. She says something to appease him, but he can't hear it. There is a loud ringing. The dark margins close over his headache to a small, square blackout.

THIS TIME IT WAS QADAR who rode the golden chain into th
man-boy. The ancestor spirit that was willed to Kifli by h
grandfather finally appeared. Just as Zulkanyan was spitefull
ignoring Kifli in his pain. Qadar slipped through the openin
of Kifli's distress. Not to wage war with Zulkanyan, only t
help, after being summoned by Kifli through a prayer on h
way out. Qadar had come to give a reprieve to Kifli
headaches. The covenant between Kifli and Zulkanyan coul
only be changed by them.

He looked at Rachel as if he had never seen her befor
She knew right away that he was not Zulkanyan. He didn
stroke his beard and the curve of his mouth had change
Qadar took the painting hanging above the bed off the wa
and set it down on the floor. He stood up in Kifli and wen
into the bathroom, where Rachel saw him spit a ball of whit
phlegm into the toilet. He undressed, shut the bathroom doo
and turned on the shower. When he came out he had a tow
neatly pleated around Kifli's waist.

Qadar put his hands together and bowed to her. '*Permiss*
He bowed again.

Rachel knew here was the real priest of Kifli's tale of go

bullets. After all, how many of them could there be? She bowed back and said the most respectable word she knew, '*Namaste.*' The nerve current in her body converging to her feet.

Qadar sat on the floor and pointed to the cigarette box. Rachel gave him a smoke. He ripped the filter off and inhaled down into Kifli's lungs. Tobacco specks stuck to his lips. He inhaled again.

The priest formed sentences by combining one word from each language: Spanish, Malaysian, Latin, French, Indonesian, Italian and Dutch. Some other languages Rachel didn't recognize. Smooth transitions of individual words from one language to the next. He knew words were a poor mode of communication. It was inevitable that interpretations would be distorted. Rachel felt their meaning. What he was getting at was that everything was connected, one language to another: a scream to a fish, a pocket of flesh to an intuition, cannibal to saint, a starving child to all the songs ever sung.

He crossed his legs on the floor and smoked.

Magic tricks are glorious when performed in a small room by a man in a towel. If this was evil, to Rachel it was also sweet fulfillment.

They sat inside a circle made of hotel towels. Qadar in Kifli's body wearing a makeshift sarong. Rachel always noticed something different about Kifli when he was absent; this time she noticed the half-heart of his calf muscle, what few black hairs he had on his toes.

They smoked five cigarettes. Kifli would never know.

Zulkanyan was always furious if he appeared when Kifli had a smoke in his hand, he'd extinguish it with Kifli's fingers.

Qadar danced inside the circle. Then he danced out of the circle and banged himself into the wall, kicked the bed frame.

Kifli's tissue salts had become accustomed to Zulkanyan's presence.

Rachel began.

'Six million.'

Qadar frowned.

'Why?'

He shrugged.

And when she continued, asking, 'Who built the pyramids?' Qadar graciously played the sound of swaying trees in her ears. White noise from God.

It was up to Rachel if she wanted to see the difference between a spirit who revealed from one who veiled. The box of pain amplifying in her chest was the answer to her quest. Qadar could do no more without waging a war that would spin Kifli&Rachel into the golden tunnel.

Just after midnight Kifli was hungry. Whenever he lost time he felt empty, so he ate to fill himself. In the grocery store they would palpate the mangoes and green kiwi fruit. More rice, eating in the middle of the night when Port Douglas was sleeping and incoming waves lingered three seconds longer, higher on the beach before rolling back.

'We have ice cream in the freezer. I saw it in a movie.' First he melted it over her eyes, then fed across her nipples and along her thighs, creating in Rachel a larger appetite.

Coming up from the beach in the morning, Rachel heard a growling dog as she crossed the neighbour's property, cutting the corner, sending off a sour scent of fear. The dog tore across the lawn to attack. Rachel hunched over to make her soft back a shell, sucked in all her spread-out particles. Everything was vivid and bright. And then the dog, its teeth already glaring at Rachel's bare legs, Rachel's skin turning red from the idea of it, stopped cold. It lay down in front of Rachel and went to sleep. It seemed to Rachel as she peered through the slats of her fingers that the dog had run into a wall.

When Rachel's shaky legs stepped into their condo Kifli wasn't there, there were only signs of him: a towel neatly hanging over a kitchen chair, a fist of cherry pits in a tea saucer on the kitchen table next to a crowded ashtray, a pack of unfiltered Camel cigarettes.

Kifli was outside on the balcony, posing for Rachel's petite Minox set in time delay. Rachel's grass hat was on his head, her sarong around his waist and her sleeveless floral Naf Naf shirt on his back. He had a cigarette in his mouth. His kris was strapped at his waist under the sarong.

The camera clicked, *shhk.*

Then she noticed Kifli had smeared her lipstick over his lips and cheeks.

'I look like you,' he said.

Rachel picked up the lipstick from the table and put a heavy coat of twinkle pink on her lips.

'We look like we belong together, anyway.' She sat on his lap. *Rachel&Kifli sitting in a tree.* The camera sent their light through a prism and gathered a solid image that will develop into a comical sight. But on the inside, at night, in the lullabies of first language, Rachel&Kifli resemble each other. And because of that, this photo could not be manipulated by Zulkanyan.

'I met someone at the bar,' Kifli said.

'You met someone? Who?'

'He called me a chink.'

She hugged him close. 'We don't belong here, Kifli.' Her chest collapsing like a fallen tent. 'Your guru hates Jews.'

'You're never going to marry me,' Kifli said.

She wiped the lipstick from Kifli's face by lifting a corner of the sarong, and when her hand grazed the kris hilt she jumped back startled. Kifli unfastened the blade from around his waist and put it around Rachel. In the next photo, Rachel is cautiously staring down and it is Kifli who is smiling. He says, 'It's mine, Rachel, he has no influence over it. It loves you like I do.' And then he adds, 'Enemies, on reputation alone, aren't really strangers, are they?'

After Kifli went out for cigarettes Rachel went to her bed, thinking, by her heavy chest, that she was catching a flu. She could smell him in the sheets—and coconut oil and ice cream and peanuts and lavender and salt. She picked up a book that had been translated from Solyums. She read excerpts from the *Undang Meleka* laws of the early fifteenth century.

*Homicide—A man can kill a paramour, a ruffian, a thief, a trespasser, someone who has run amok.*

Kifli slid into the Central Bar. Clapping his bare feet down on the wooden floor. The local tattoos watched.

*While involved in a fight it is not unlawful to kill someone who interferes in the fighting.*

He recognized the guy who had insulted him earlier, who then said as a general comment to the bar's patrons, 'Now the slant's a Sheila.'

*A drunken man is not held responsible for his behaviour. If he dies, his host is fined. If he can't pay he will be carried round the city accompanied by the beating of a gong.*

Kifli lit a cigarette.

*A thief can be killed on the spot.*

In a vision, he saw this man hauling in a fish net. And he saw a long, eight-foot shadow running up his arm. When the man realizes he is strung by the grey cords of a box jellyfish he will cry for his mother. Hollow tubes, driven by a nature smaller than the head of a pin, will explode wandering venom through his veins. He will die in cardiac arrest with a seven-foot trail of the sea wasp leading back into the water.

*A Muslim should not be killed for killing an infidel, or a father a son, or a freeman a slave.*

Kifli judged the man as weak as a decapitated chicken. He passed him like a cool wind and ordered a beer, as if he was any other patron in the bar.

Kifli took a mouthful, swished it between his teeth, held it as if he might spit it out, then, in slow time, Kifli Talib swallowed the first alcohol of his life. By the time Rachel tracked him down it was late. She took one look at him, laughing with new friends, waving his cigarette in the air. 'Jesus, Kifli.' She held her hand over her heart. A shallow inhale. *I am full of smoke.* Her flesh was grating on rocks and Kifli was gulping beer. She clung to the back of Kifli's chair. Before she could steady herself next to him, she fell, slowly to the ground. And landed as a puddle, like they do in the movies. She looked up at Kifli, who staggered to pick her up. In a bar, where most of the people were possessed by alcohol, no one even noticed the Malay man-boy dragging the Jewess, half on her feet, out the door, the two of them balanced on a thin kris blade.

Kifli turned away to vomit at the side of the road. What

could she do with him now that he was drunk, crying and puking, gagging on alcohol—muscles weak and soul divided. Saying her name. Laughing and crying. He kept his arm around her waist. Even when he stepped out to the side of the road to heave again, he pointed one arm back at her. 'Listen to me, Kifli, I can't take care of you.' She was hoping Zulkanyan would take over.

Zulkanyan was there. Kifli wouldn't let him in. 'What are you going to do?' Kifli said to him, 'Kill me.'

'You have taken her this far, you have agreed. Don't accuse me,' was the reply.

Rachel no longer saw the path. She was inside her laboured breathing—a grey-black fog. She had to get back to the room, to sleep. The only other thing she remembered before she blacked out was the calmness. After Kifli carried her up the stairs, into their room, placed her on the bed, she said without resistance, 'I'm dying.' Happily. Peacefully. Nothing was better or easier.

Breathing blue smoke from her box of pain.

Kifli watched a vapour encircle Rachel, her white face glowing through the haze—a still and porcelain cheek.

'Take her,' said Zulkanyan. 'Strangle her.'

'She isn't mine to take,' said Kifli.

'Of course she is.'

'She isn't yours either.'

Kifli had never tried to revive someone he was killing.

He had never killed someone he loved.

Zulkanyan rang a retched scream into Kifli's ear and bit the Malay man-boy so hard on his brain Kifli could only sense shadows hanging around the room. Was Rachel dead?

Her lips were black-ruby, like a sacrificed goat's tongue. Her eyes empty. Her cold hands withdrawn.

There I was with Rachel suspended in my arms ready to guide her to the golden spiral. Her loneliness, her fluidity had come to know, through Kifli Talib, how to travel at the speed of light. So she left.

She was ready to abandon this world, and when she did, Kifli Talib begged for her back. His kris in his hand and some arsenic to go with her.

I held her. Her soul was a hologram floating in the middle of the room.

Until a piddly little sound came from the cold girl. A string of words that turned into a seed from an apple tree and fell to the ground. *With his consent I shall speak of mysteries.* Kifli wanted to swallow the seed. He wanted to drink it. He also knew it was not for him. He handed it to me. I saw my wife Rachel.

*Water soothes with its shields those swollen souls. Rain forces revive, as a tree planted on a stream is protected. Saved from fire and water.*

Rachel as if she had been inside of me all these lonely years.

A flash of light.

RACHEL GOLD OPENED HER EYES to Kifli Talib staring into her face, screaming, 'Are you all right? Are you all right?' Wailing. 'Please be all right.'

'What is it, Kifli?' His voice dragged her up from everything.

He lifted her neck and kissed her lips. Fat tears fell from his eyes onto her cheeks.

'Shh, go to sleep.'

'Rachel, talk to me. It's such a mess. The room is such a mess.'

'Take your clothes off and come to bed.'

'Rachel, please.'

'Kifli.'

'I'm afraid.'

'Don't be silly, come to bed.'

He rushed to the end of the bed, grabbed her feet and rolled them vigorously between his hands. He kissed her heels as if they were holy shrines. So it seems.

'Kifli, are you awake?'

'I'm here, *Sayang*, what do you need?'

'I don't know.'

Rachel is blowing like a snapping flag.

'There's a sweet smell in the air,' she says.

'Yes.'

'I'm so light. I'm a hundred pounds lighter. I feel like my insides have been taken out and washed. Especially my lungs. My body has been to the laundromat. Ha. What did you do to me? I can fly, Kifli, I have wings.'

'I'm happy you feel better.'

'Are you kidding? I'm a new person. It's gone.'

'Yes.' He began to cry again. 'Yes, it's gone.'

'No, no, you don't understand, I was dying and now it's gone.'

'I'm so happy.'

'You don't look it.'

'I'm tired. I'm happy, Rachel, believe me.'

'I was dying.'

'Don't say that.'

'But I was and you know it.'

Looking down at Kifli sitting on the bed, Rachel bent awkwardly over his shoulders, then swung her legs around his waist. Kifli gripped the end of the mattress, held himself upright as she shimmied onto his lap. He had those hands that wanted her but would never reach out on their own, no matter how much he desired her. She puzzled at the stamina of his distance and, simultaneously, his complete presence.

He said, 'I would be a hero if I killed you.'

Rachel put his arms around her naked back, but she couldn't feel them because he was holding her so serenely.

'We don't ever have to leave this room,' she said.

'I *sayang* you,' Kifli cooed. The sound of him made her body wild tangerine—blue pits beating inside. Above Rachel a door opened and as she breathed, a warm wind, not sweet but green, came into her head. In slowtime Rachel floated like a leaf, comfortable, blissful, in her own skin.

'Death,' she said, 'is nothing to fear.'

# Book III

Time is a liar—it is a thief. A dreaded road we walk along without choice. A road that is essentially unknown. We are beggars of time. We want more. We want less. In youth we are untouchable, immortal, with no sense of time. Later, bemoaning wasted hours, we cast off inhibitions, sometimes ending in the place where we started—some marked beginning, before any time had passed at all.

RACHEL WOKE UP IN THE MIDDLE of the night with the acute perception that she had been reliving the same day for months. Years? The last time the world had slipped into slow time, she was peering over her shoulder at the Malay man-boy. Not smiling, not frowning, hardly breathing, almost not standing where he was, almost sprinting back into her arms for one more second of slowtime tenderness.

In the heart of that night Rachel thought she was going to die of loneliness. Even though she had a career and went to lots of dinner parties, had a good hairdresser and a hand-sewn Paul Smith coat she had brought home from London, she was dying of loneliness. Then there was Kifli in her dream making love to her. His hair like pink silk, where she could see her younger reflection.

She felt like she used to, like she was under water. Back then Kifli was too. Only he was fossil-infested and had no room inside to accommodate the new world. Years ago, Rachel knew how to time-travel, so she headed down his ancestral past looking for treasure. Stones to pile up and stand on so she could ascend the waterline and breathe.

*March 21, 1997*
*Dear Lennart,*
*I am leaving for Singapore in a few days. You will understand I must go back, as you went back to Asia and found your nervous breakdown. While I was trying to get rid of my demons, I also lost the better part of myself. I want to get some of that back. Maybe if I find Kifli…*
*How does one distinguish herself from her own imagination?*
*Be well, my friend.*
*Rachel*

In her journal she enters a list of her magical talismans, in case she needs them for a defence.

*The first cuttings of the flight feathers of a lovebird chick*
*Papyrus*
*Lucky stones*
*Pink nail polish*
*Love letters*
*Monkey face ceramic eggcup*
*Medicine pouch*
*Troll doll with human hair*
*Italian glass angels*
*Nana's wedding ring*
*Dad's snubnose Smith & Wesson*
*Kifli's Pantun poem*

*Coral from the Red Sea*
*The birth announcement of Dana's twins*

Then she writes, *When I was young, Kifli was my lover and he had my water and my psyche in his body. And my water drowned his guru.*

Rachel arrives in the heat of a Singapore evening. Through the bus window on the way to the hotel, her reflection is divided by tree shadows and lamplights. She wonders if Kifli knows she is there. Or if she is safe.

She is unnerved by the relocation of the front drive of Raffles Hotel, and then they inform her that they have no rooms that have not been renovated. 'Falling apart,' as the front-desk clerk put it. The Hermann Hesse suite is no longer noted by a bronze plaque and its room number 107 is now 114. Rachel thinks the room has become just another hotel room in Singapore with a stain on the carpet.

She dumps her suitcase out on the floor looking for the photo. The picture of what it was to be in a magician's air—invisible, unaccountable to anyone. Her only evidence that this story exists. Kifli had set the camera on the television set and pressed the thirty-second delay. In the picture she is a mere veil of skin, a transparent outline. A ghost against him. She is sitting on Kifli's lap and you can see him right through her. A flock of birds fly through her head from the painting on the wall.

Wide awake in Raffles Hotel at four in the morning, knees to her chest, she's rocking in bed. Rachel dreads that she might never know who Kifli is. There isn't enough time if she has all the time in the world.

She claims him, legs crossed over a feather pillow while imagining Kifli out of control, throwing his ecstasy in all directions, an afternoon downpour. Air conditioning forced into damp, hot, slightly musty air.

Kifli is driving home. When Rachel cums his throat tightens briefly. This is how she sees it; he would never tell. After so much time, they are unknown to each other, and as familiar as the starlight coming in through the hotel window.

That night all their dreams are in Tibetan red.

Ten fathoms into the underworld, having tea and scones, while others lilt into cellphones. At the mouth of the Raffles City station reading *The Straits Times*.

> *Up to 2000 Johor youths taking Ecstasy pills. Paloh Chong Ah Owon of the National State Assembly wants the racial breakdowns of students involved in crimes over the past three years.*

The people in the morning take the steps from the underground, dressed primly, as demanded by the state. Ties hang from white shirts. And to the West, and to the rest of Asia, their hearts are singing, 'Ha, ha, we all have jobs, we have apartments, wealth without democracy of substance.' Revamped for the techno-future with leadership crying, 'Kill the chicken to teach the monkey.'

Hundreds of worn-out shoes beat the red stones of the sidewalk in front of the metro. Sculptured bushes brood under trees nearby. Hard morning sun nags at Rachel. The taste of unexplainable sterility in the air is the meat of a thousand meals. She feels so full. She is looking for one who has his frame or his hair. Even from the birds and trees she sees elements of Kifli: a coy eye, a rigid bark that has become saturated with humidity. There is no order. There is a mirror. In the mirror the face is a stranger staring back, asking, 'What about the murders?'

Just like any other day, a young woman has a seizure and hits her head on the pavement. The wind blowing the leaves sounds like a thousand warm eggs cracking.

Kifli kept writing, begging to come to Toronto—*get me out of this place, I can't survive here, I can't survive without you.* When she didn't reply, his handwriting became almost illegible. A single word on each line.

*I*

*am*

*your*

*servant*

The last letter she sent to him was brief.

*Dear Kifli,*
*Here is some money to replace your broken spectacles.*

She finds Kifli Talib's name in the phonebook.

He tells her his father died in October after a long illness. That he commutes from Singapore to Malaysia between the future and the past, hired by a Japanese company to plant coconut trees for shade on golf courses. Is her hair still long?

He speaks as if he still knows her, not realizing she has matured within her own country. In the compass of other men. He says he's not surprised, he's been waiting.

'Where are you?' he says.

'At Raffles.'

'I'm coming.'

She doesn't recognize him, only knows his voice from the recording he sent her of him singing a Malay love song. Kifli wears a gold chain around his neck, sways back and forth cool on his feet.

He says her full name, Rachel Lynn Gold, and then he calls her *Sayang*.

The memory of how she came to know him is vague. *He waited for me under the veranda in the rain. In the corners of buildings he looked like a flickering idol, standing dry behind the lazy weather.*

His arms open.

His two hands already resting on her hips.

Rachel inhales him, making a full recognition. Pulls back to see he still has the sad eyes of an opera.

He is bloated like a body that has been floating in the river. Inflated, his scars might be stretched to form a word or a map under his shirt. She tries to see him the way he is but her image of him is younger, the way he was when he was structured like a Siamese cat.

He pushes off her hips, clicking his head to the left, looking into her face. He says, 'I forgot to ask if you were married.'

'No.'

'Someone must be wanting to take you.'

'It's not that.'

'You've changed,' he says. 'You're stronger. You're stronger than me.' He smiles. 'Zulkanyan's gone. We're alone.'

'I've come only for you,' she says. 'There's so much I've forgotten. Kifli, I've forgotten who I am.'

He says, 'You're not asleep anymore.'

'And you, you're so...'

'Fat, I'm so fat.' He bows his head. 'I married a Chinese girl. She's a good cook. She works for IBM.'

Rachel's water pulling toward him like moon tides filling the cracks of her lips. Irrational and lush.

'I don't like the renovation,' she says. 'Raffles isn't as brave as I remember it. The only thing they kept was the chinaware and the silver.'

He says, 'I haven't been here since you.'

So many years apart, they can't speak about their love, so they talk about the island of Singapore as if it is their passion. All built up. The speed of the city, so fast, so expensive, thousands of Singapore dollars for a pass just to drive on the downtown roads. A receding jungle with increasing heat load and floods. Poison spiders. What happened to his knee? Two operations and a limp. He goes on about the water sources of Malaysia and why the farmers are setting fire to their own fields, because it is cheaper than farming them. The people are starving. He agrees it's a good thing to do.

'How was your night?' she says.

'It was long.'

'Mine too. It was so long.' She continues, 'You're lucky you have a wife to sleep with.'

'I slept on the couch.'

'I didn't sleep at all.'

'My wife doesn't know about Zulkanyan. And you?' he says. 'Why didn't you sleep?'

'Probably the time change.'

'It's possible.'

He sits behind the wheel of a borrowed car. A blue Toyota. His car is a wreck and he doesn't want Rachel to see it. He's wearing cologne. One hand on the steering wheel, the other in her lap, he says, 'I'm just a man now. I could blow Zulkanyan over with a whistle if I wanted to.'

'Where are we going, Kifli?'

'Just for a drive.' The car motor is hissing. Kifli flicks a lighter, *shhk*. His vowels drag. Everything he says has the high pitch of a question.

'I was never afraid of you,' she says. 'It wasn't you. You were the safest place in the world.'

Kifli smiles. 'You're still living it. It still owns you.'

Rachel opens the glove compartment. Full of maps folded inside out. She sees the straight between Singapore and Malaysia, and then territories she has never been. There is a flashlight at the back and some keys.

'I have a right to know what happened,' she says. 'I'm not the same.'

He says it back to her, 'You're not the same.' Then he says, 'Let's just be human. You know the Muslim and the Jew were born from the same tree.' Then he tells her a riddle the children at the kampong had told him. '"You know how a fish moves?" they asked. I said, "A fish moves this way." "How about a stingray?" I said, "A stingray moves that way." "Do you know how a fish moves this way and that way but not at all?" I said I didn't know. Do you?'

Rachel shakes her head no.

'The fish trapped in the net cannot move at all.' He turns the car onto a highway. He adjusts the rearview mirror. 'You were walking around without direction,' Kifli says. 'You come back full of direction but no further ahead.'

'I guess you don't wear my bangle anymore,' Rachel says.
'I lost it.'

'Where are we going?'

'I thought you'd like a drive. You never saw much last time.'

At a stoplight Kifli pulls a bead of cotton from the crotch of his pants. 'After you left,' he says, 'Zulkanyan began shouting profanities at my mother during her prayers. My mother, who is second after God, said I was no longer her son. I should go to the guru and cleanse the Jewess out of my heart.

'I told her the guru was full of rotting words. "Hate the prostitute, hate the Jew, hate the infidel."

'She was at the kitchen table ironing my father's work pants. I took the iron from my mother's hand and pushed it into my arm and screamed, "I'm not your soldier, Zulkanyan."

'My arm was bubbling up and smelling of burning flesh. I don't remember diving down the stairs, but I did.

'When my father returned from his ship we went to see the *bomoh*. The kampong was fluttering with children. They made me dizzy. I held my father's arm the way you used to cling to me. The *bomoh* cut open some limes, tossed them against a wooden board. He said, "A Muslim doesn't want to speak to spirits. I can show you the way, Kifli, the rest is up to you."

'He ordered a lot of my things to be taken away from me. Burned all the clothes Zulkanyan liked. I had a tooth from a tiger, an amulet to wear in troubled times given to me by my guru. Seven or eight stingray tails with the poison still in them, crocodile private parts for energy, wood from trees and little pieces of string and cloth. The *bomoh* also took my cobra skin that was peeled off when it was still alive. Everything was thrown into the sea through a river. Except some ears in a glass vile I had hidden in my mother's closet with earrings attached to them. A blood-stained silat costume. Skin. Everything was thrown into the sea. Even my kris. Your bangle went too. And a bit of my blood. I lost time. And whenever I woke up there were four or five strong men ready to tie me down. I stayed in the fishing village for nine months. Living the old way without cars or friends. Zulkanyan was struggling to stay with me.

'At the end there was a ceremony where I had to call him. When he didn't appear it meant my doors were locked. It took four years for me to get rid of him.'

Kifli takes both hands off the steering wheel and raises them to his shoulders as if someone is holding a gun to his back.

'After that I refused to go to a mosque, or to the guru who kissed me on the lips when he wanted Zulkanyan. I've become a non-believer who would happily take shelter under a Jewish veranda, even if it wasn't raining.

'People came to my mother's house with money in their hands. "Come on," they said, "your son is a bridge, he's a rope, he has a ladder in his head worth dollars." Not worth all the money in the world to me. I told my mother that if I added up all the time I'd lost, I could live another life.'

Rachel fumbles in her purse and pulls out the photo. 'What about this?'

Kifli lights a cigarette, says, 'You were a weak spirit and the camera took you as you were.' He stubs the cigarette out. 'Come on,' he says. 'Why do you act so innocent when you can bring Zulkanyan out whenever you want. My guru couldn't do that. He sweated for hours. You just called

"Oh Zulkanyan," and he came. He wasn't supposed to be nice to you.'

Kifli slides his hand into his trouser pocket, pulls out a small tin of cough drops. They shake like a shaman's rattle. He opens the lid, extracts a dusty lozenge, pops it into his mouth. 'Zulkanyan would have to brainwash my feelings to get me to hate you.' He smacks and sucks, moves the pebble about; it grates on his teeth then settles under his tongue. The obstacle makes his slurred words sound accusatory. 'You should have told me you were speaking to him from the beginning.'

'Some people are doomed,' Rachel says. 'Do you think that is what's happening to us?'

Kifli doesn't answer.

'It's not something I can decide alone,' she says.

Kifli's breathing like a motor car idled at the side of the road. He takes the pack of cigarettes from his shirt pocket. Passes a cigarette to Rachel. 'My kris was in their hearts.'

Silence.

'Did he tell you to do it?'

'You know that.'

'Where did you put their bodies?'

He says, 'Do I still look like a boy to you?'

'No.' She says it right away, insistent. 'No, not at all.'

He can hear her unsteady breathing too. She says, 'Maybe we can start again the way things are now. There's so little time.'

Kifli has exited the highway. He pulls into a parking lot. Rachel reads 'Sony' on the building.

Kifli's hands are gripping the steering wheel. 'I had to put my love for you somewhere, so I gave it to my wife. But it's your love.'

'Oh.'

They're in the scorching heat, in the exaggerated bright-
ness of the day. Here in this parking lot Kifli holds her almost
without touching her.

'Oh.'

Her constricted heart unshackles. Because Rachel Lynn
Gold believes in his love. Kifli Talib's love. Because she has
harboured him. Because he knows her. Because for this
moment they both agree to suspend their suspicion. She
allows herself to surrender instead of submit. And at exactly
the same time, he also allows himself to surrender.

A man and a woman.

Kifli's love for Rachel given and accepted.

There was no Zulkanyan or Qadar. I too was excluded
from their union. Time passed slowly through the seconds of
the digital clock on the front of the building. Time did pass.
And it also stood still. Briefly. The sky was a field of trilliums.

She does not kiss him. Occasionally, their lips meet. She
is aching to merge in sleep. For now, the blue Toyota car
drives back onto the highway.

'The *bomoh* threw the limes. He said I love you more than
your future husband will. I love you second. There was someone who loved you more.'

And when Kifli says to her that he would still be a hero if
he killed her, a Jewess, Rachel laughs. 'Why would you do
that? Now that you've finally saved me.'

Kifli tilts his head abruptly to his left shoulder. He sighs.
The unpaved road is bumpy. It's getting dark. At the side of a
dirt path women wearing sarongs and T-shirts are lifting
sticks and thrashing them down on coarse straw bags. Thick
red stains are seeping through the canvases.

'Dragon's blood,' Kifli says. 'Colouring from a rattan fruit. It's used as dye for Chinese lacquer.'

Kifli lights a cigarette. He hands it to Rachel. She inhales then rests it in the ashtray. Kifli takes one hand off the steering wheel and inches it into her lap. The clouds look like ceiling fans. 'See? It's going to rain.'

Rachel pushes her hands to the car window and peers out.

# Author's Note

THIS NOVEL TAKES PLACE in the 1980s and the first draft of this book was written before the unfortunate events of September 11. It could seem now that Rachel&Kifli existed at a distant time, but their attraction is so insular and personal that I suspect they would have come together in almost the same way today. I say *almost* because love is vulnerable to the judgment of the world.

The character of Uncle Joseph was inspired by the Indian actor David Abraham, or 'Uncle David' as he is known by many, who is most famous for his movie *Boot Polish*, which won him a Film Fare award for best supporting actor in the early fifties.

The ghost of Garnet Warren is rendered from a ghost that hung around my family's farmhouse at Knights Beach when I was a child. The Gold family is not my family. Rachel's Dunnville is not mine. Rachel's Singapore is her own.

Much primary research went into the writing of this book during time spent in Singapore, India, Nepal, Australia, Israel and Canada.

*Raffles: The Story of Singapore,* by Raymond Flower, provided the quote for the title. Sir Winston Churchill referred to Singapore as 'The Naked Island' when it fell so quickly to the Japanese during the Second World War.

*Emotions of Culture: A Malay Perspective,* edited by Wazir Jahan Karim, shed light on much of the information I acquired during interviews that took place in Singapore in 1997.

*An Analysis of Malay Magic,* by K. M. Endicott, and *The Malay Magician,* by Richard Winstedt, were most valuable in my research into Malay culture. Some lists for magic spells are taken from *Malay Magic,* by William Skeat. Also thanks to *Taming the Wind of Desire: Psychology, Medicine, and Aesthetics in Malay Shamanistic Performances,* by Carol Laderman.

Useful sources on the sacred Kris knife include: *The Kris: Mystic Weapon of the Malay World,* by Edward Frey, and *The National Cultural Encyclopaedia: The Kris and Other Traditional Indonesian Weapons,* English translation.

For history and geography, I am indebted to *A Descriptive Dictionary of the Indian Islands and Adjacent Countries,* by John Crawfurd, F.R.S., *The Biophysical Environment of Singapore,* by Chia Lin Sien, and *Grand Heritage,* Dunnville District Heritage Association.

My appreciation to the following works quoted in this novel: William Blake's *Jerusalem,* written in 1820; a passage from Rabindranath Tagore's novel *Gora*; excerpts from the *Undang Meleka* laws of the early fifteenth century; and the Pantun poem from *Malay Pantuns* by A. W. Hamilton. The Thangka painting described in Shrinigar came from

*Sacred Buddhist Painting*, by Anjan Chakraverty. The prayer for the rain and the prayer for dreams were drawn from a translation by Zohar Able of the traditional Hebrew prayers.

My gratitude to the Raffles Hotel for their generous attention. I am grateful to all these sources and any faults are my own. While the author has made every effort to trace the owners of copyright, she will be happy to rectify any errors or omissions in future editions.

# *Acknowledgements*

MY FATHER WOULD BEGIN many evenings at the dinner table with 'When I was in Russia...' and stories about how his pet monkey tried to strangle my grandmother, and how my grandfather got a parking ticket for conducting the opera while driving, expanded my imagination into a vast and minute universe that includes everyone. My father, of course, had never been to Russia. My deep appreciation to my dad for opening the door to the world with awe and for always being there, so I have never been alone. Thanks to my mother, who inspired me to find my voice, and who let me stay home from school when I didn't want to go. Gratitude to my sister Jamie, who has forged ahead of me and paved a path to admire, and to Rob Held for the love he has brought to our family. Thanks also to my brother David, for taking care of the office while I was dreaming, and to Darlene Shapiro.

Ruby, you made me want the world to be a better place. And it is, with you.

Thank you to Anna Porter, Publisher of Key Porter Books, for believing in this book. My gratitude to my editor Janie Yoon for being a beacon that I was able to trust. I am grateful to Marjan Farahbaksh, for treating the manuscript with generous sensitivity during the laborious task of copy-editing. And thanks also to the entire staff at Key Porter, including Lyn Cadence, Meg Taylor, Sheila Evely, Peter Maher and Brad Kalbfleisch.

My writing circle—Michelle Hammer, Netta Rondinelli, Collette Yvonne, Joy Barber—read numerous drafts of the manuscript and helped enlighten the writing process. Special thanks to Maria Coletta McLean, who probably knows every word of this book by heart for all of the work she has put into it. And for all the love she has put into me. I am also grateful to Janet Looker for the labour and birth coaching of this book and Ruby. A bond beyond words. Ann Shortell, whose remarkable generosity of spirit and outstanding advice in every aspect of this book, has been a pillar for me, her devoted friendship a reprieve. This book would not have made it without her.

Paul Hanson, Ph.D. of Folklore and Anthropology, provided insightful comments on the text, and much needed late-night humour. My gratitude to Kevin O'Leary, my dear friend and office partner, who for three years tried to walk carefully up the office stairs at two in the morning without making me jump with fright, and who has been there from the beginning. Thanks to Joanne Sack for her assistance with the copyedit and for always being just around the corner.

My appreciation for assistance with research and translations to Sherry Ciccodemarco, Victor Abraham and Kartini Rivers.

Thanks to Michael Eames, who assisted me with permissions from the estate of Bob Marley; Justin Poy for generously providing me a space to work in along the railway tracks; Sandra Panagopoulos and Bill Panagopoulos for a place to clear my head; and Lawrence Camaya for his speedy computer support. Fond thanks to Steve Paikin for taking me through the media ropes and for setting the standard for first dates in grade eight.

I never would have sustained the task of writing this book without the encouragement of teachers and fellow writers. Thank you: Brian Wylie, for taking me into the world of literature with such passion; Don Summerhays, who told me to read women and who made me explain why I repeated the same word three times in succession in a poem; Susan Swan, for being a one-woman circus and for conducting her class accordingly; Dionne Brand, who inspired me with her honesty; Bruce Powe, for his interest in and caring of my work; Lucy Hall, who imparted so much good sense and was always in the best mood; Sarah Sheard, for her good advice and support to the very end; Etti Naveh, who 'unstuck' me at a critical point; David Layton and David Margolick for their generosity; and Michael Posner for believing in me and for his good company. Thank you also to Malcolm Lester, who was the first to read the final manuscript and whose encouraging words carried me through the gruelling process.

The years fly by and these friends have stood by me to my good fortune: the late Nettie Levine, the late Shirley Levy, Brinah Levine, Suzy Zucker, Herb Solway, for his good council, Tina Goldlist, Hershey Piafsky, Neil Pichora; Arlan Mintz, thank you for being someone I can trust and for never doubting that I could. Thanks to Leslie Arnold, Amy Hunter, Ashley Gracile for often carrying my burdens, Yana Kay, Steven Ding, Ira Liebtag, Lisa Turner, Mark Kuper, Svika Raz, Tova Raz, Avrum Rosensweig, Michael Silverman, Per-Anders Karlsson—the best tour guide I ever had, and who remains my heart's keeper. My sincere gratitude to Mary-Ann Metric, Lori Noble, Josie Sferrazza, Menachem Kammer for your reverence, Pete Weston, Gabrielle Nagler, Sidney Williams for taking care of me when I was down on the mat, Jan Nathanson, Yvonne Roberts, Deborah Wasserman, Norbert Kausen, Efraim Ritter, Marilou Tabulog, Donna Levy, Lena Ginsberg, Joel Ginsberg and Dave Jones. Thanks to Dewith Frazer for all these years of appearing at my door with his strong shoulders; Zohar Able for bringing light into my house and of course her good cooking; Michael Spicer for being there every second when I was vulnerable and restoring my faith; Lotta Strandman for our walks; Kjell, Jim and Nicole for all the years at Alpvägen; and sincere thanks to Steven Arnold and Gian Luca Orienti. My gratitude to Rachel and Alan Goldberg, who took me into their home and family years ago in Melbourne, Australia.

For the healing of Body and Soul, my gratitude to Mirium Erlichman, Ricardo Harris, Margaret Kirk, Silvia Jacobs, Ted Saito, Kieth Cammacho, Mirium Jacobson and Lynda Kerby. Gloria Doyley for your loving good care and safety.

And to the Malay man-boy, my Muse.